SHELBY & WATTS

A Mountain of a Problem

by ashlyn anstee

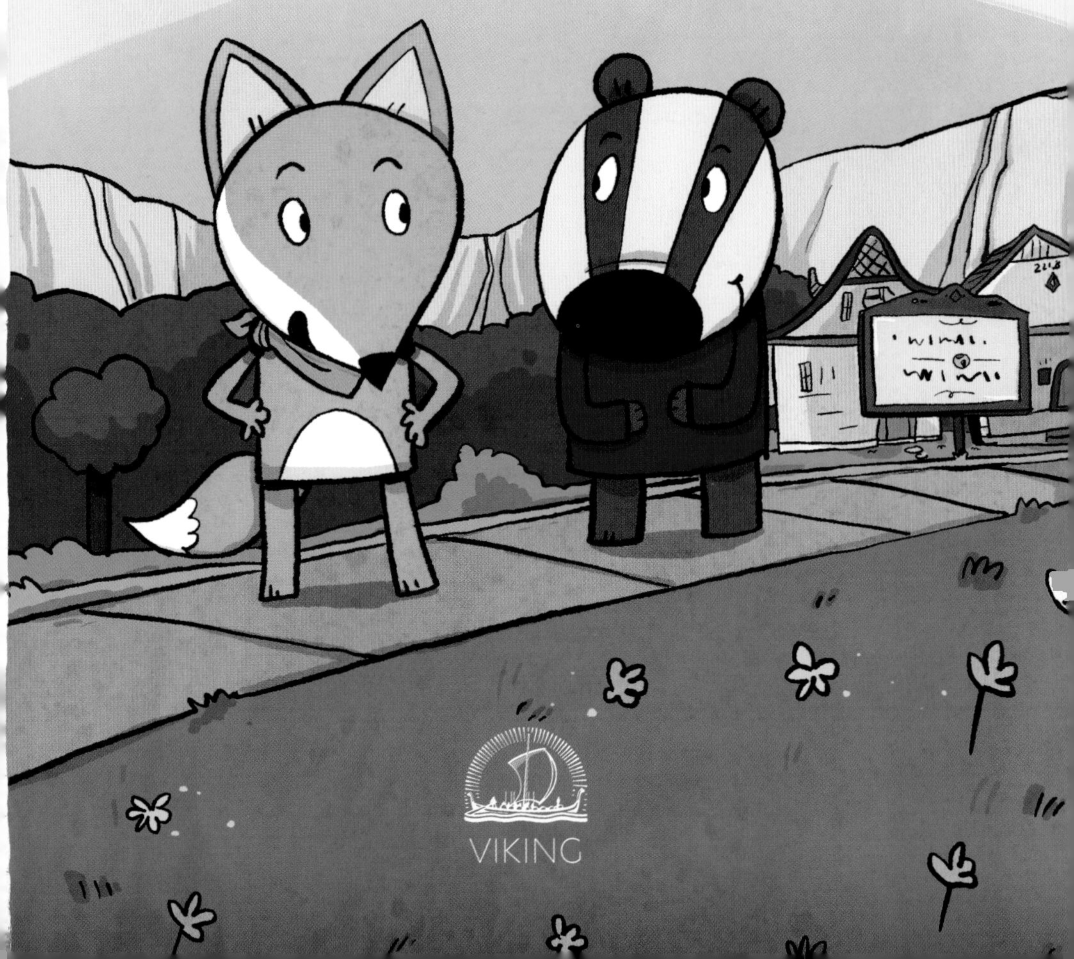

VIKING

For Grandma, love you always.

VIKING
An imprint of Penguin Random House LLC, New York

First published in the United States of America by Viking,
an imprint of Penguin Random House LLC, 2022

Visit us online at penguinrandomhouse.com.

Library of Congress Cataloging-in-Publication Data is available.

Manufactured in China

ISBN 9780593205358

1 3 5 7 9 10 8 6 4 2

TOPL

This book was drawn in Procreate and Photoshop on an iPad,
with a few little watercolor textures here and there.

CHAPTER 1

In the village of Valley Glen . . .

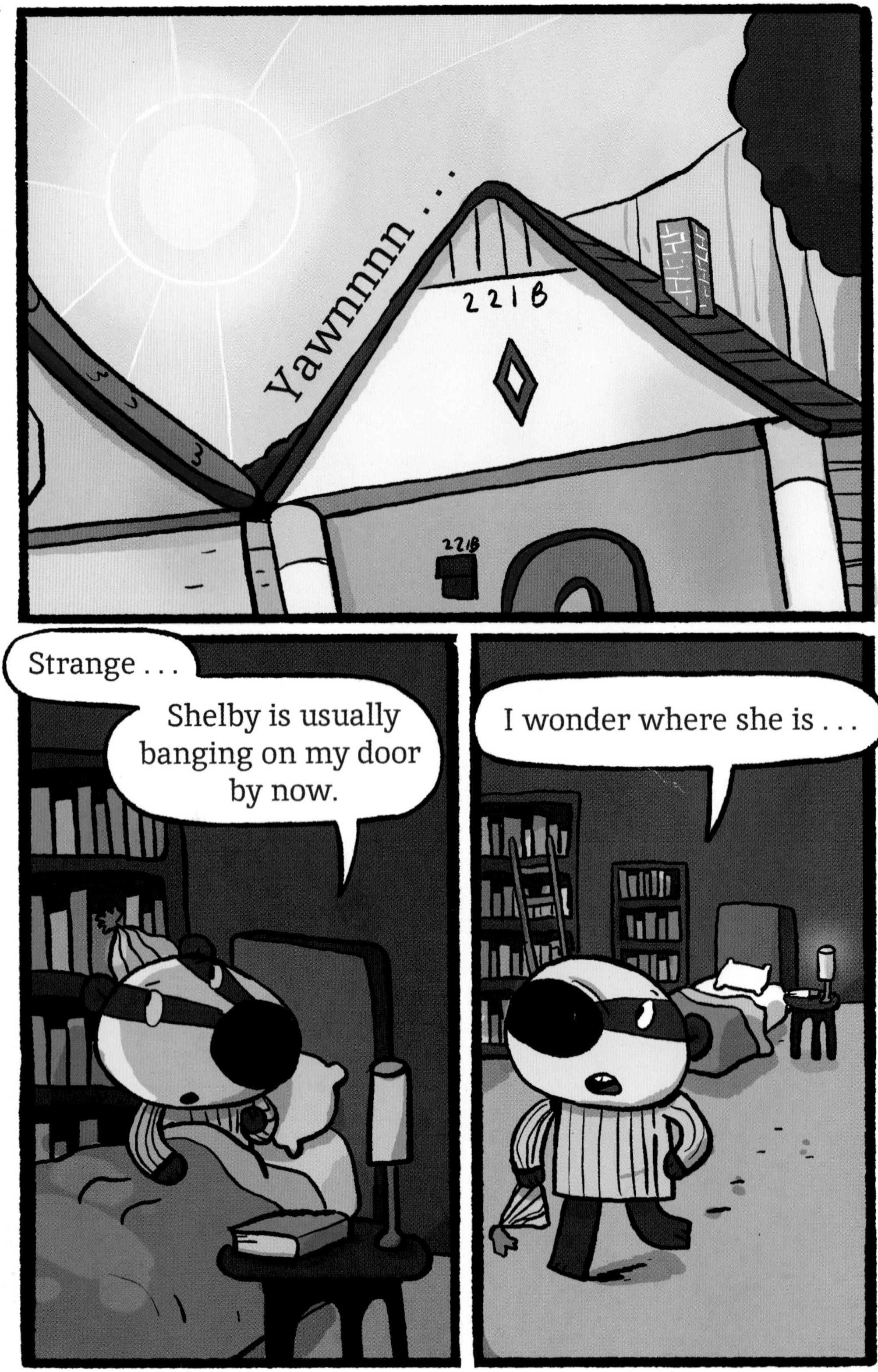
Yawnnnn . . .
221B
221B
Strange . . .
Shelby is usually banging on my door by now.
I wonder where she is . . .

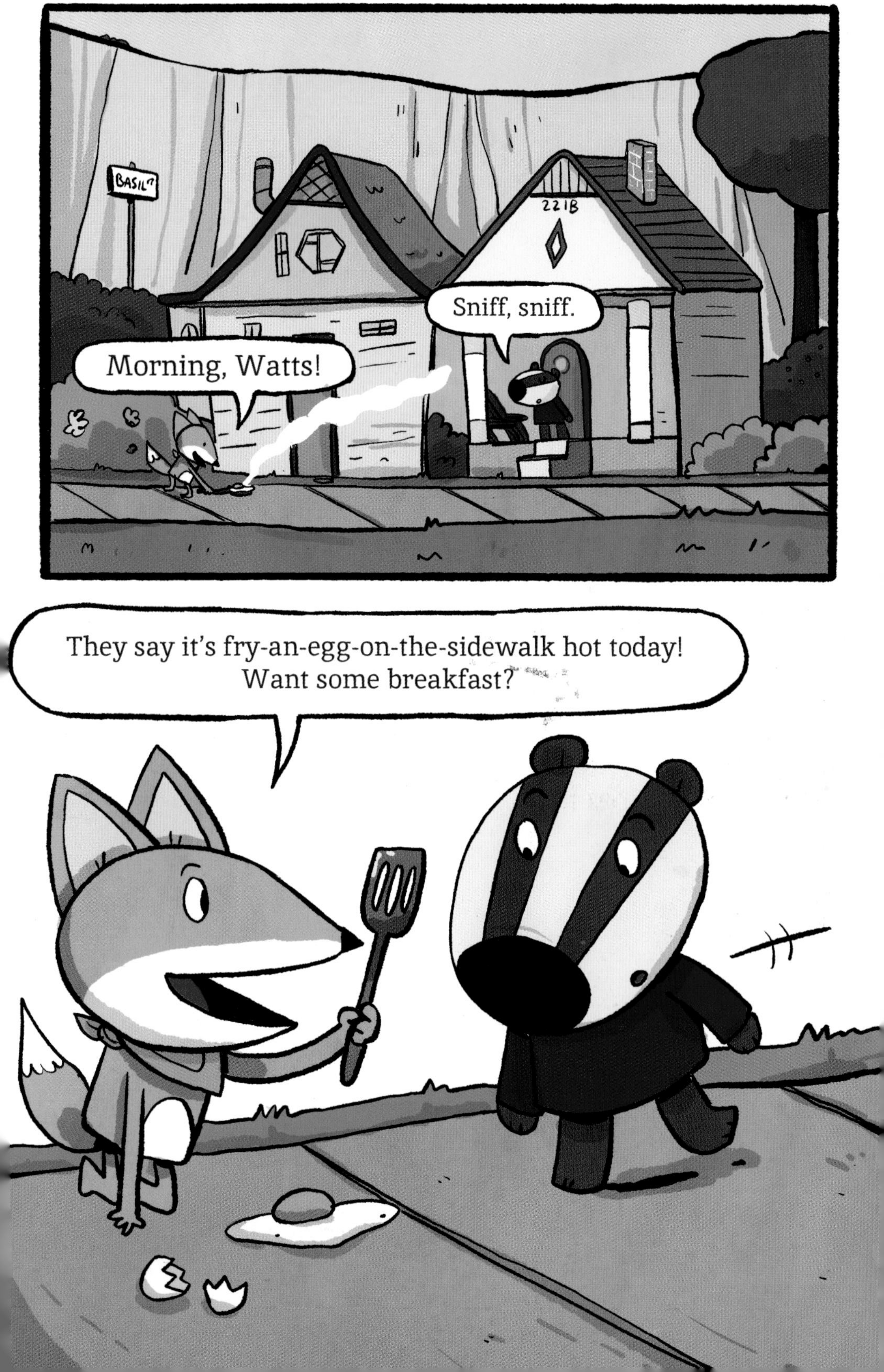
BASIL
221B
Sniff, sniff.
Morning, Watts!
They say it's fry-an-egg-on-the-sidewalk hot today! Want some breakfast?

Planetary Investigators
Shelby & Watts

fox

Job:
Lead Detective
favorite snack:
jelly beans

badger

Job:
Researcher
favorite snack:
cheese

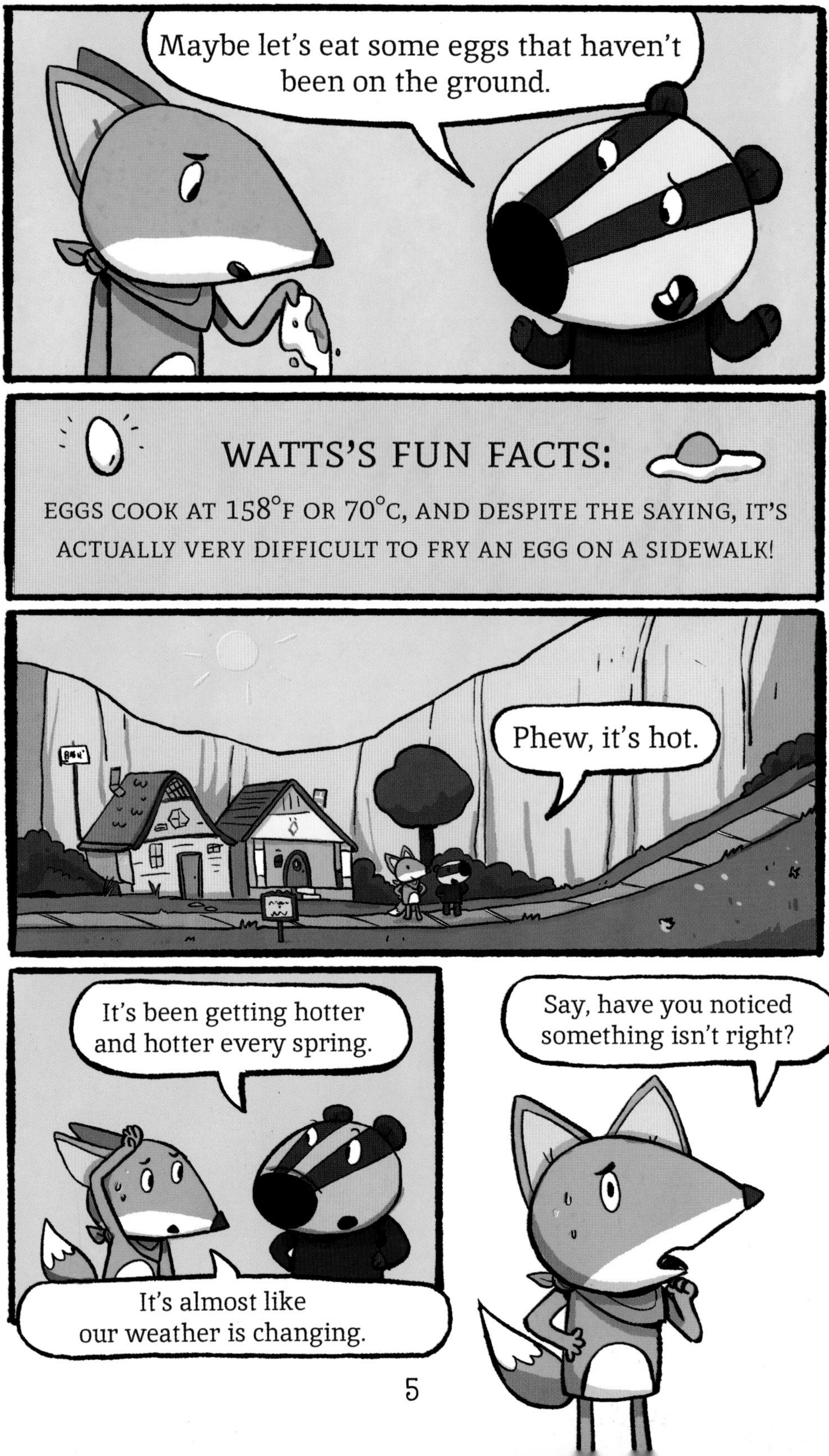

Maybe let's eat some eggs that haven't been on the ground.
WATTS'S FUN FACTS:
EGGS COOK AT 158°F OR 70°C, AND DESPITE THE SAYING, IT'S ACTUALLY VERY DIFFICULT TO FRY AN EGG ON A SIDEWALK!
Phew, it's hot.
It's been getting hotter and hotter every spring.
It's almost like our weather is changing.
Say, have you noticed something isn't right?

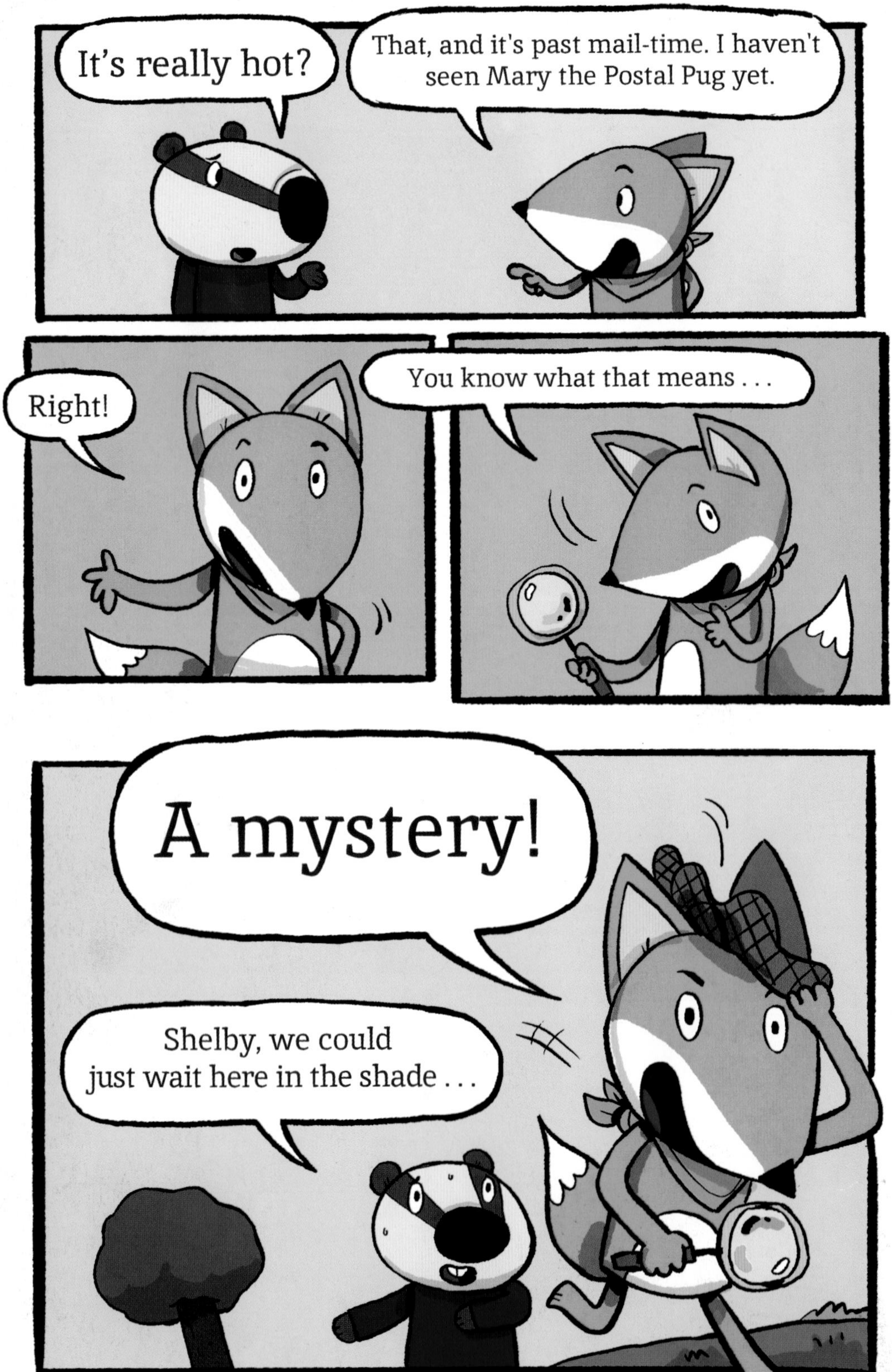
It's really hot?
That, and it's past mail-time. I haven't seen Mary the Postal Pug yet.
Right!
You know what that means . . .
A mystery!
Shelby, we could just wait here in the shade . . .

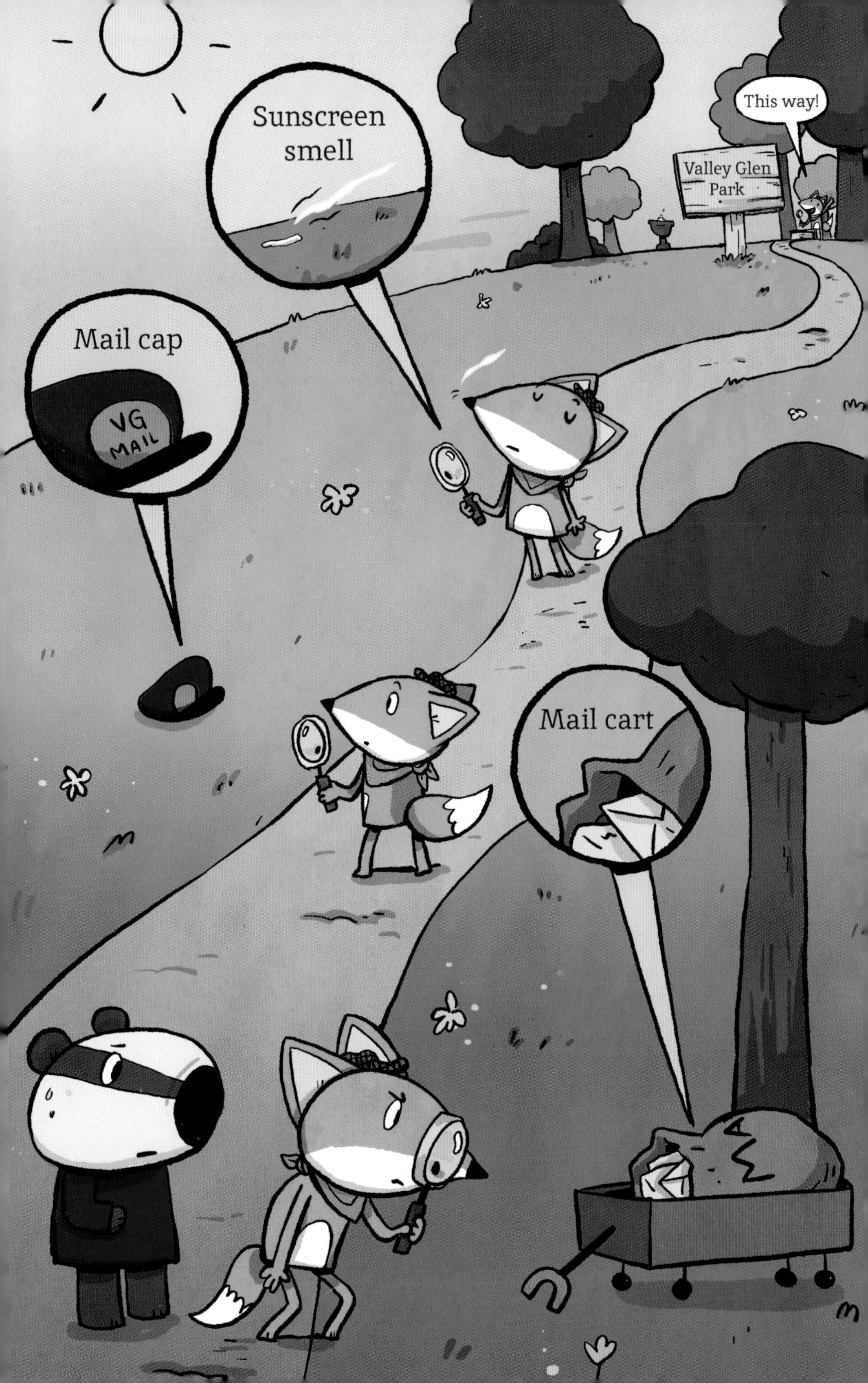
This way!
Valley Glen Park
Sunscreen smell
Mail cap
VG MAIL
Mail cart

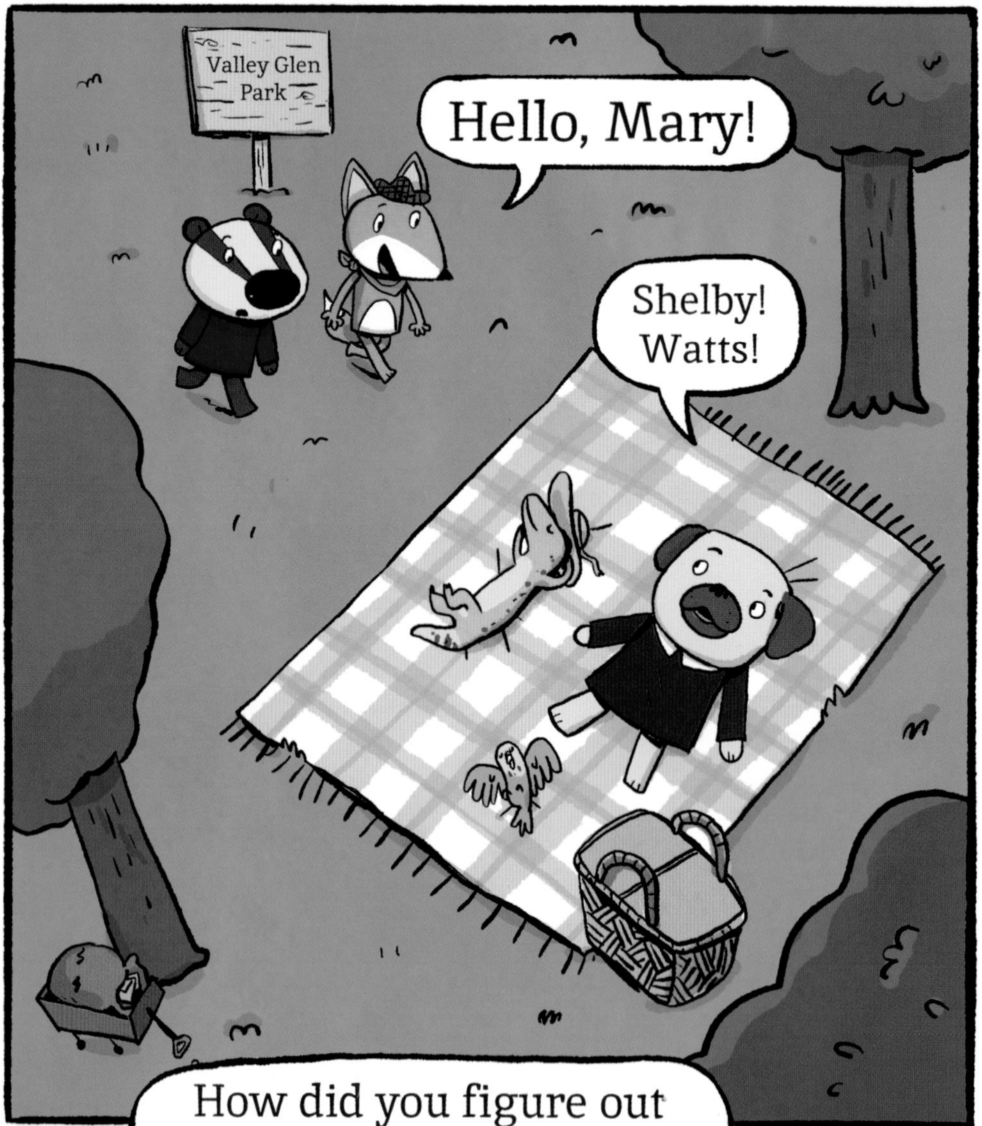
Valley Glen Park
Hello, Mary!
Shelby! Watts!

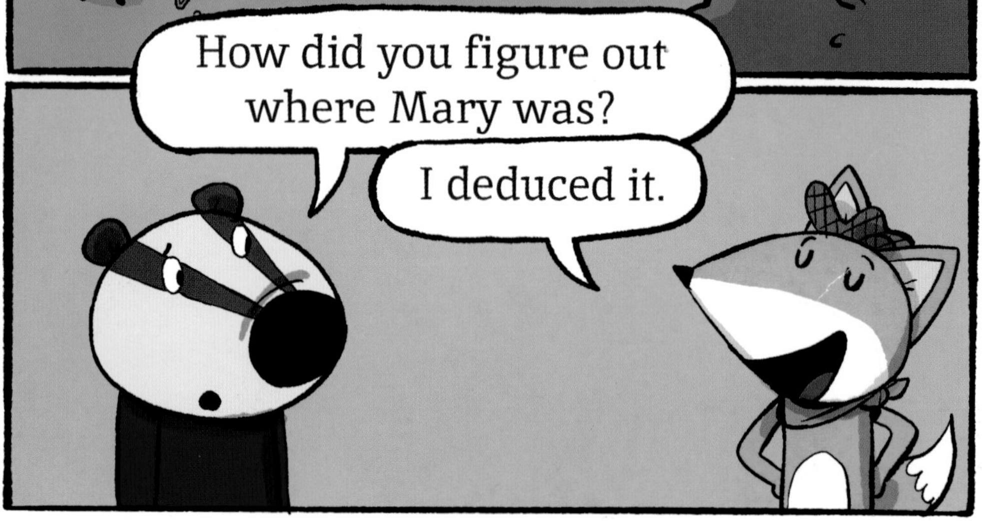
How did you figure out where Mary was?
I deduced it.

The Case of the Missing Mail-Pug

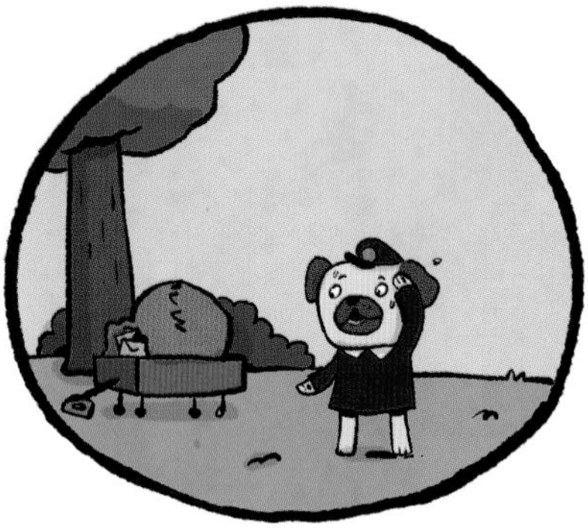

The mail cart was tucked safely behind a tree.

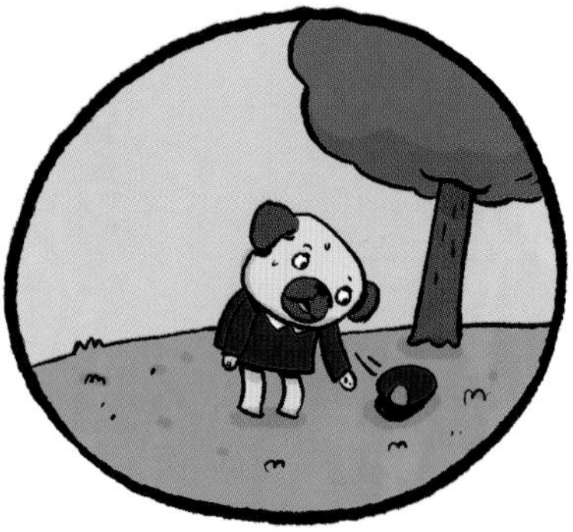

A few steps away, I noticed Mary's mail cap.

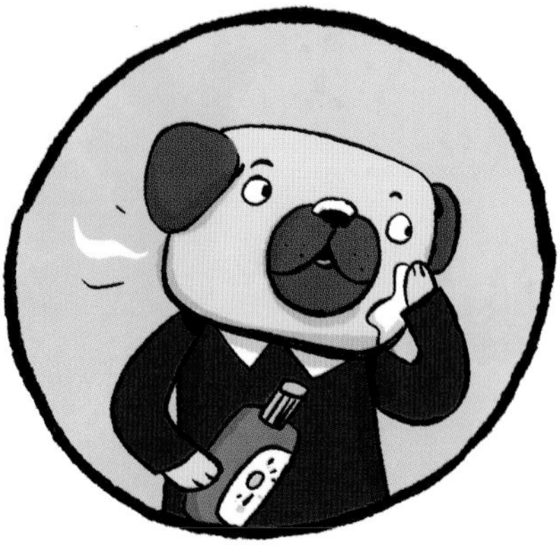

I smelled freshly used sunscreen! That meant she must be close by.

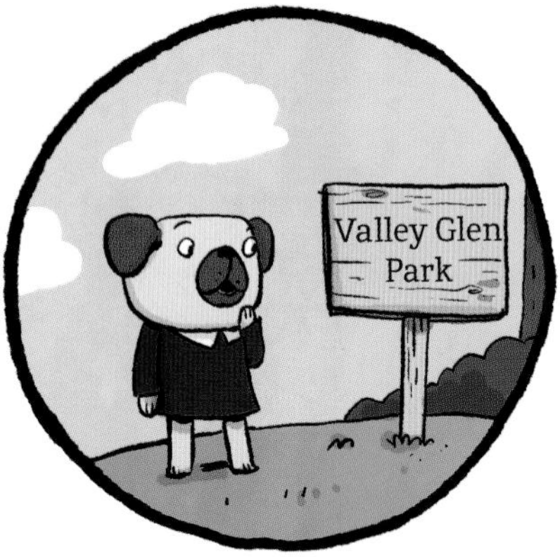
Valley Glen
Park

These clues were just steps away from the best place for a picnic in Valley Glen . . .

Deduction: Mary is at the park!

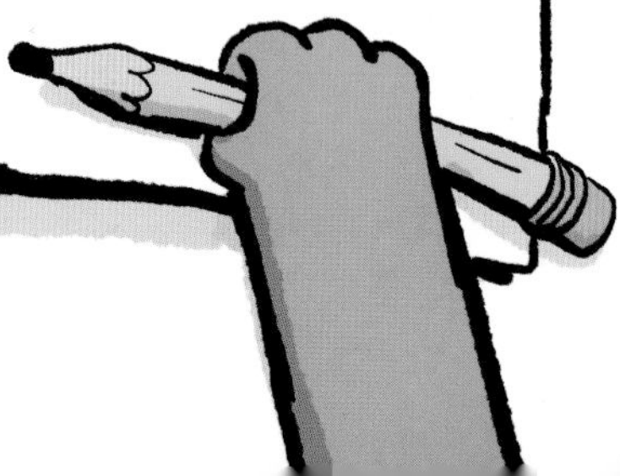

Solved!

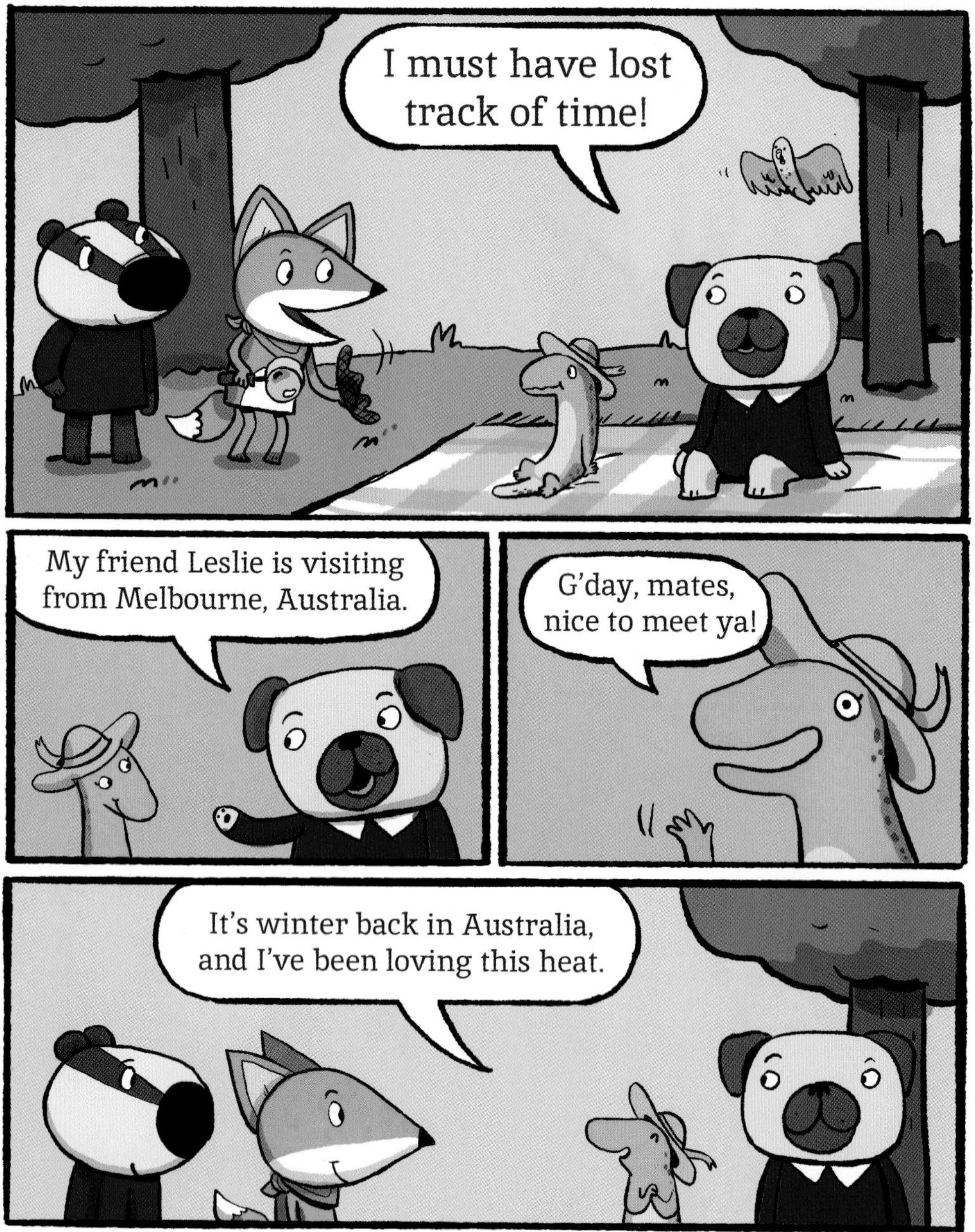
I must have lost track of time!
My friend Leslie is visiting from Melbourne, Australia.
G'day, mates, nice to meet ya!
It's winter back in Australia, and I've been loving this heat.

THE SEASONS IN THE NORTHERN AND SOUTHERN HEMISPHERE ARE SWAPPED.

IF IT'S SUMMER IN THE NORTHERN HEMISPHERE, IT'S WINTER IN THE SOUTHERN HEMISPHERE!

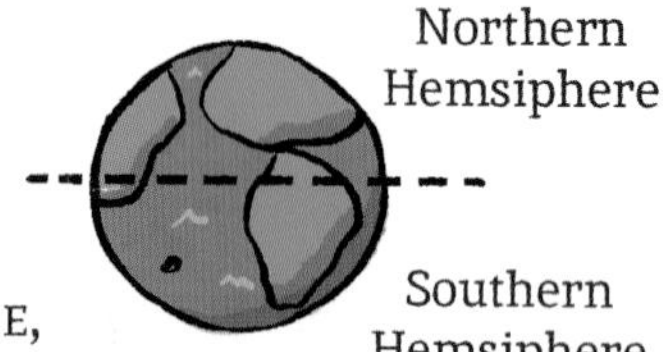
Northern Hemsiphere
Southern Hemsiphere

Leslie

gecko

Job:
Business Owner

favorite season: summer

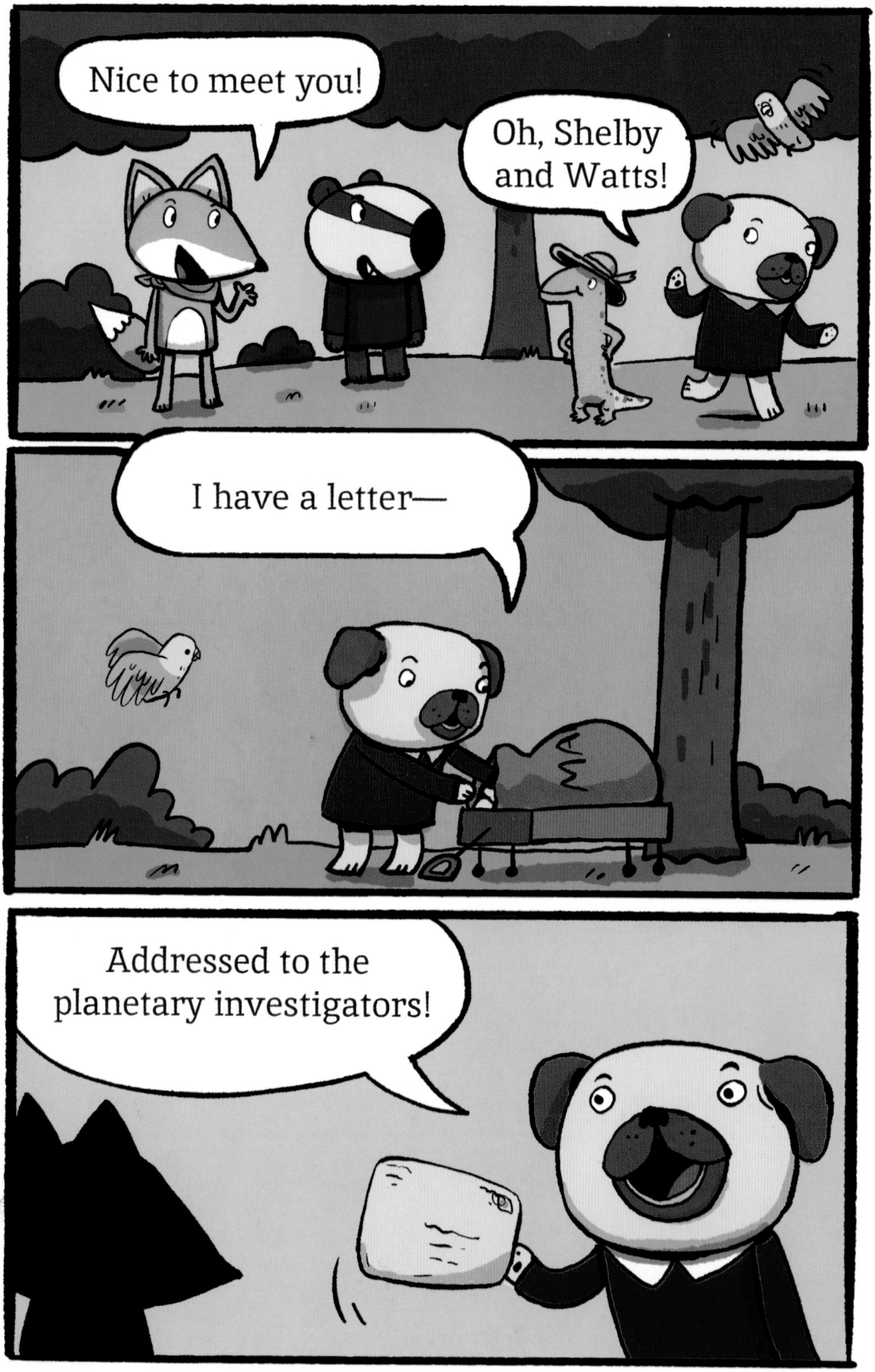
Nice to meet you!
Oh, Shelby and Watts!
I have a letter—
Addressed to the planetary investigators!

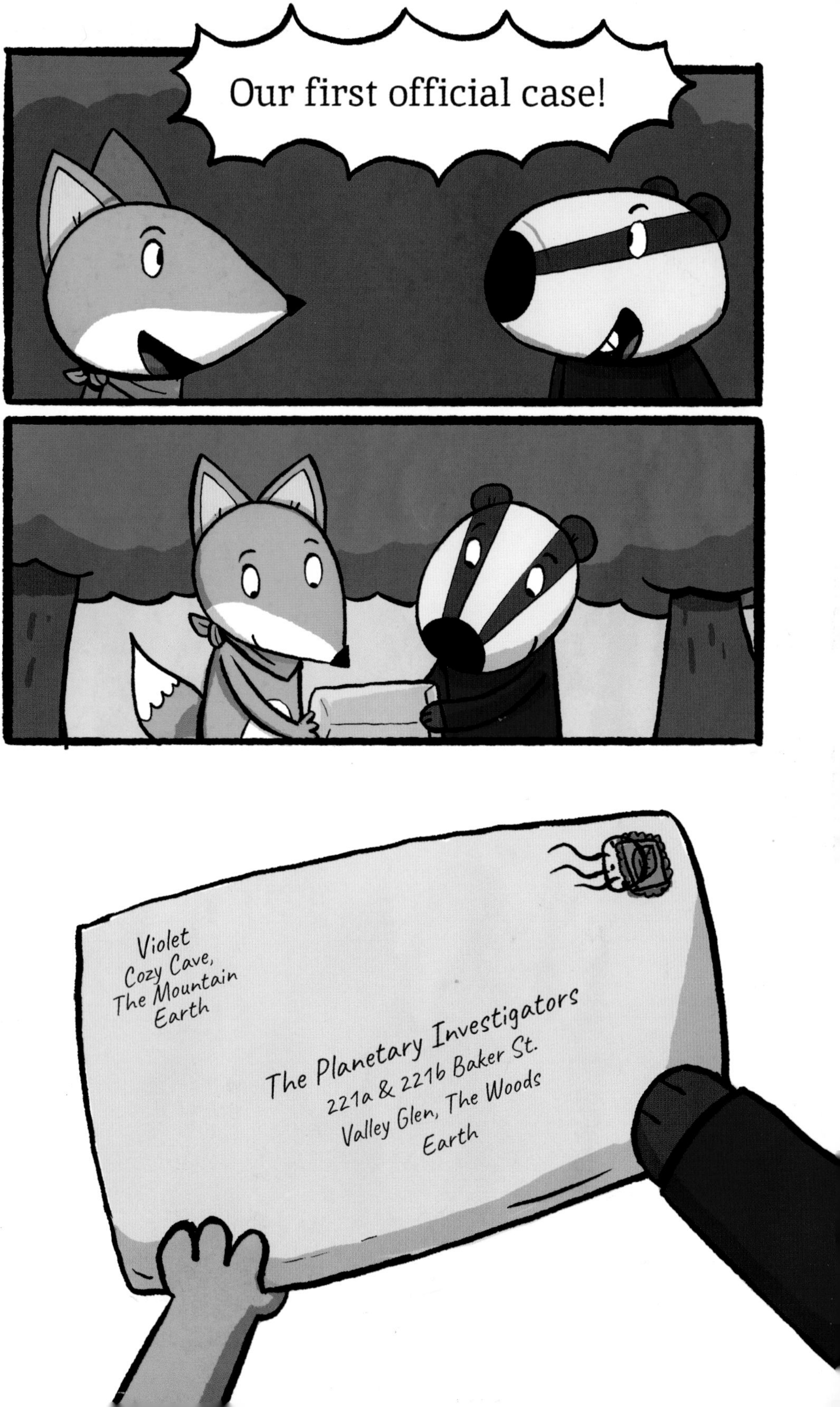
Our first official case!
Violet
Cozy Cave,
The Mountain
Earth
The Planetary Investigators
221a & 221b Baker St.
Valley Glen, The Woods
Earth

Detectives Shelby and Watts,

  Sorry for my sloppy handwriting. I'm quite sleepy.
  My name is Violet, and I'm a black bear. I live with my cub, Theodore, in the mountains.
  My friend Mary told me you run a detective agency.
  I need your help.
  I just woke up from hibernation . . .

  Early!

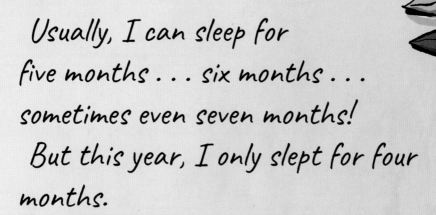

   Usually, I can sleep for
five months . . . six months . . .
sometimes even seven months!
   But this year, I only slept for four
months.
   If little Theodore wakes up, there
might not be enough food ready for
him.
   Will you help me figure out why I woke
up so I can keep Theodore asleep?
   I'm really grasping at straws here!

                    Violet

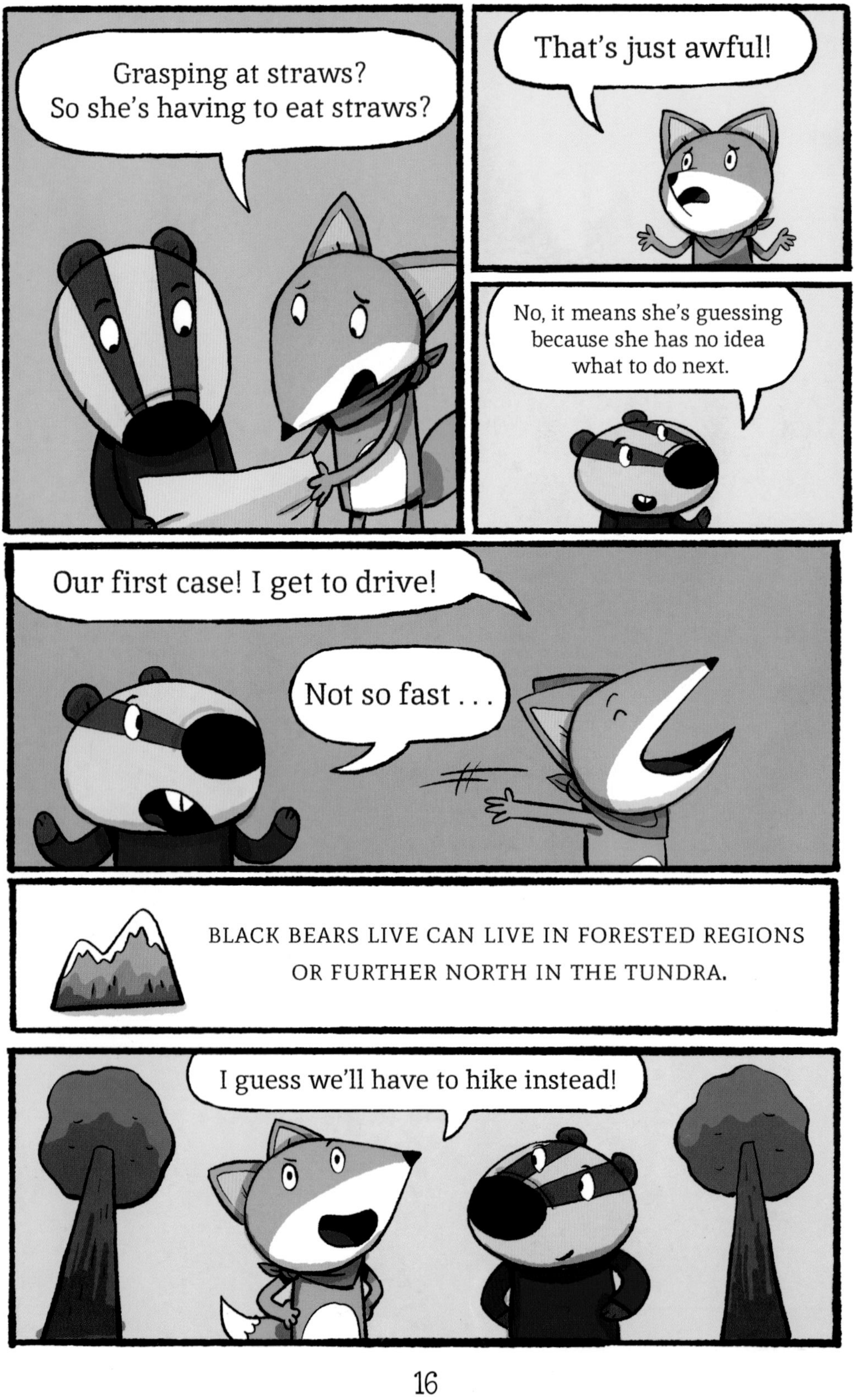
Grasping at straws? So she's having to eat straws?
That's just awful!
No, it means she's guessing because she has no idea what to do next.
Our first case! I get to drive!
Not so fast . . .
BLACK BEARS LIVE CAN LIVE IN FORESTED REGIONS OR FURTHER NORTH IN THE TUNDRA.
I guess we'll have to hike instead!

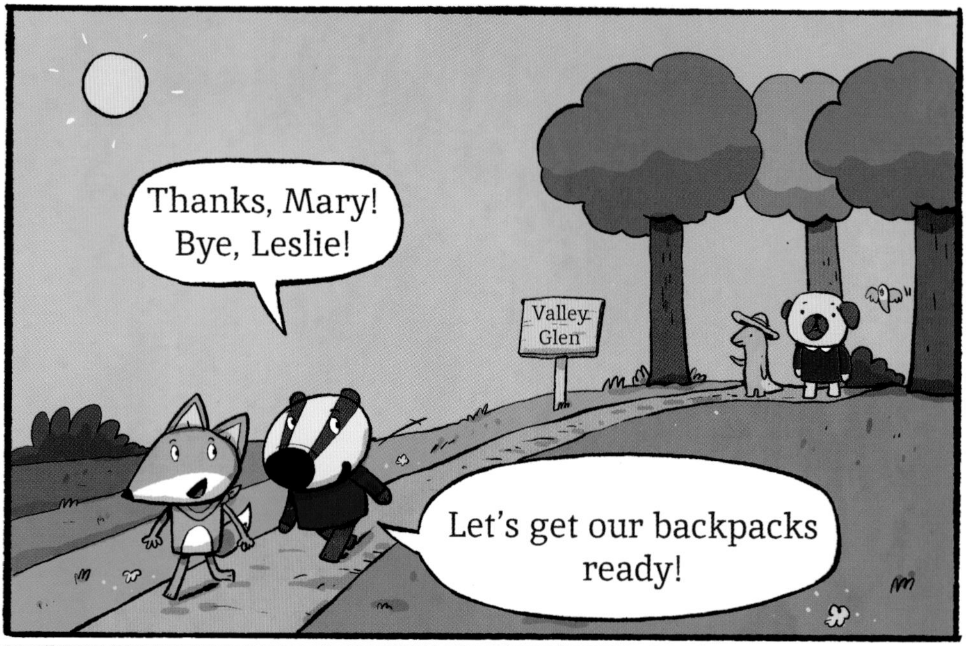
Thanks, Mary! Bye, Leslie!
Valley Glen
Let's get our backpacks ready!

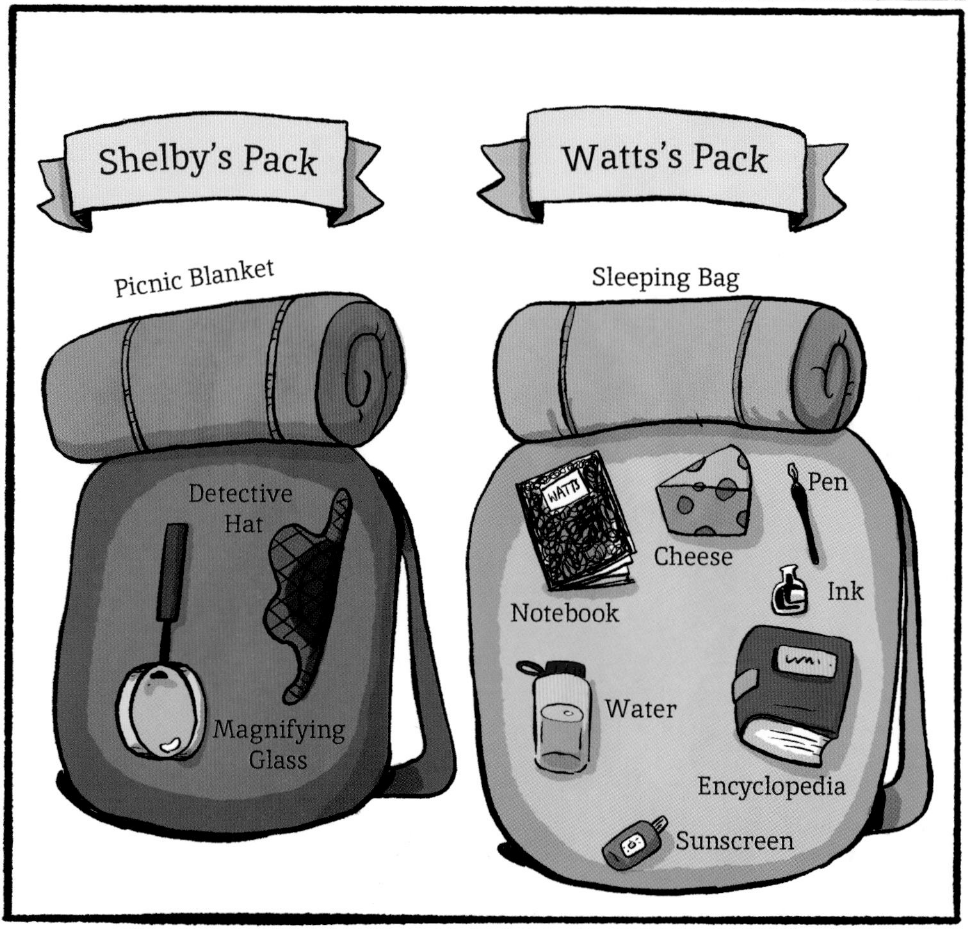
Shelby's Pack
Watts's Pack
Picnic Blanket
Detective Hat
Magnifying Glass
Sleeping Bag
Notebook
Cheese
Pen
Ink
Water
Encyclopedia
Sunscreen

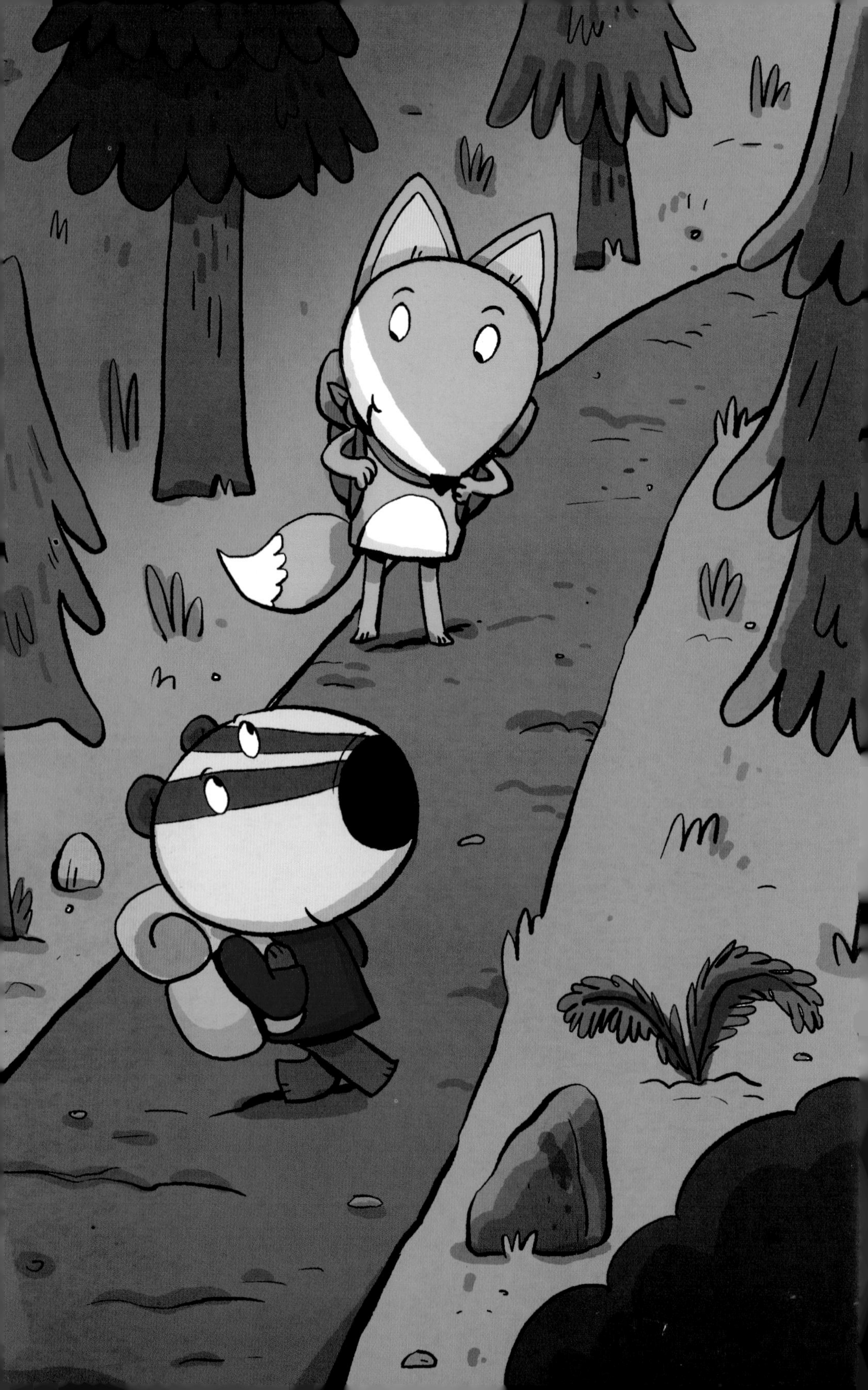

CHAPTER 2

In the mountain forests . . .

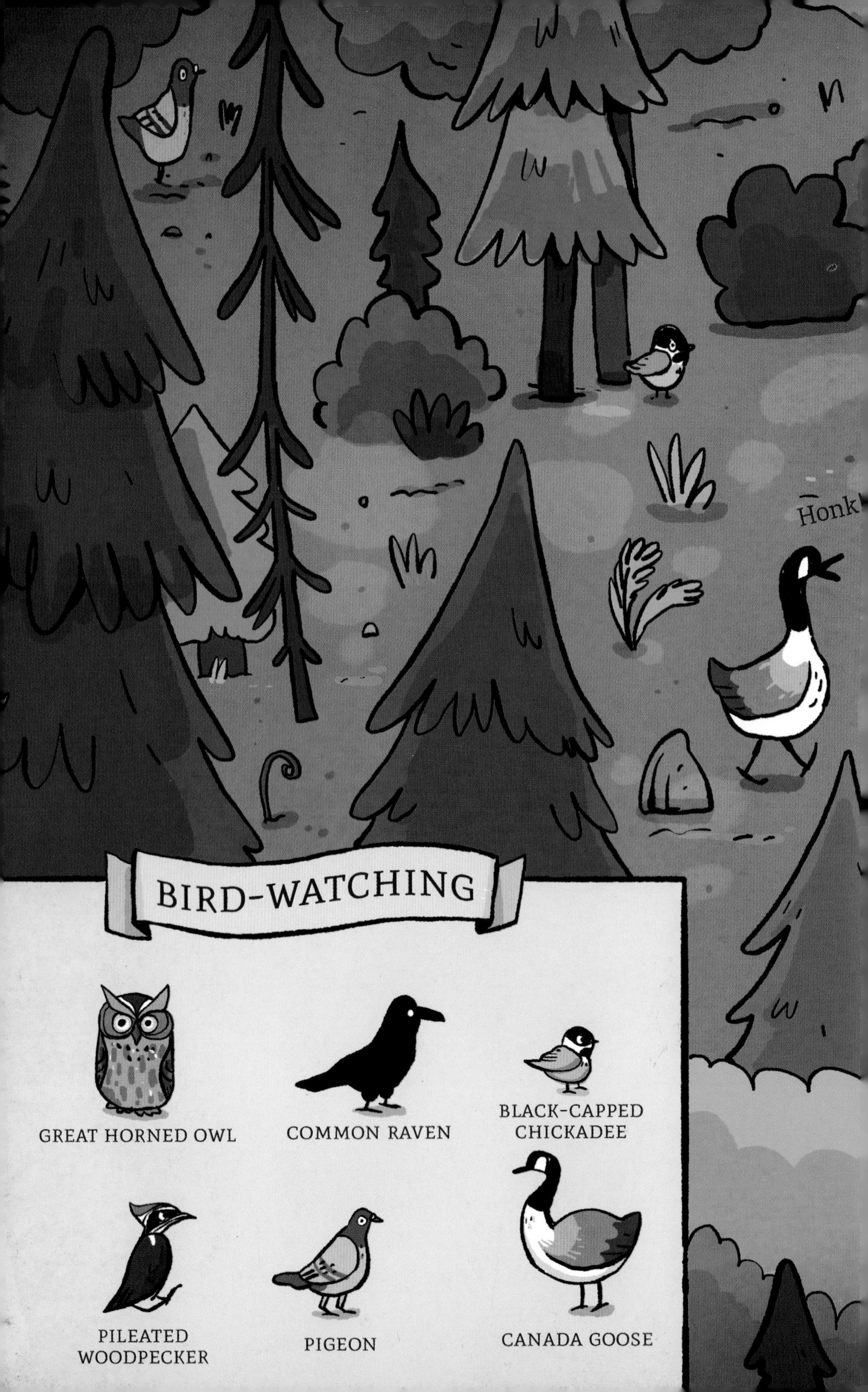
Honk
BIRD-WATCHING
GREAT HORNED OWL
COMMON RAVEN
BLACK-CAPPED CHICKADEE
PILEATED WOODPECKER
PIGEON
CANADA GOOSE

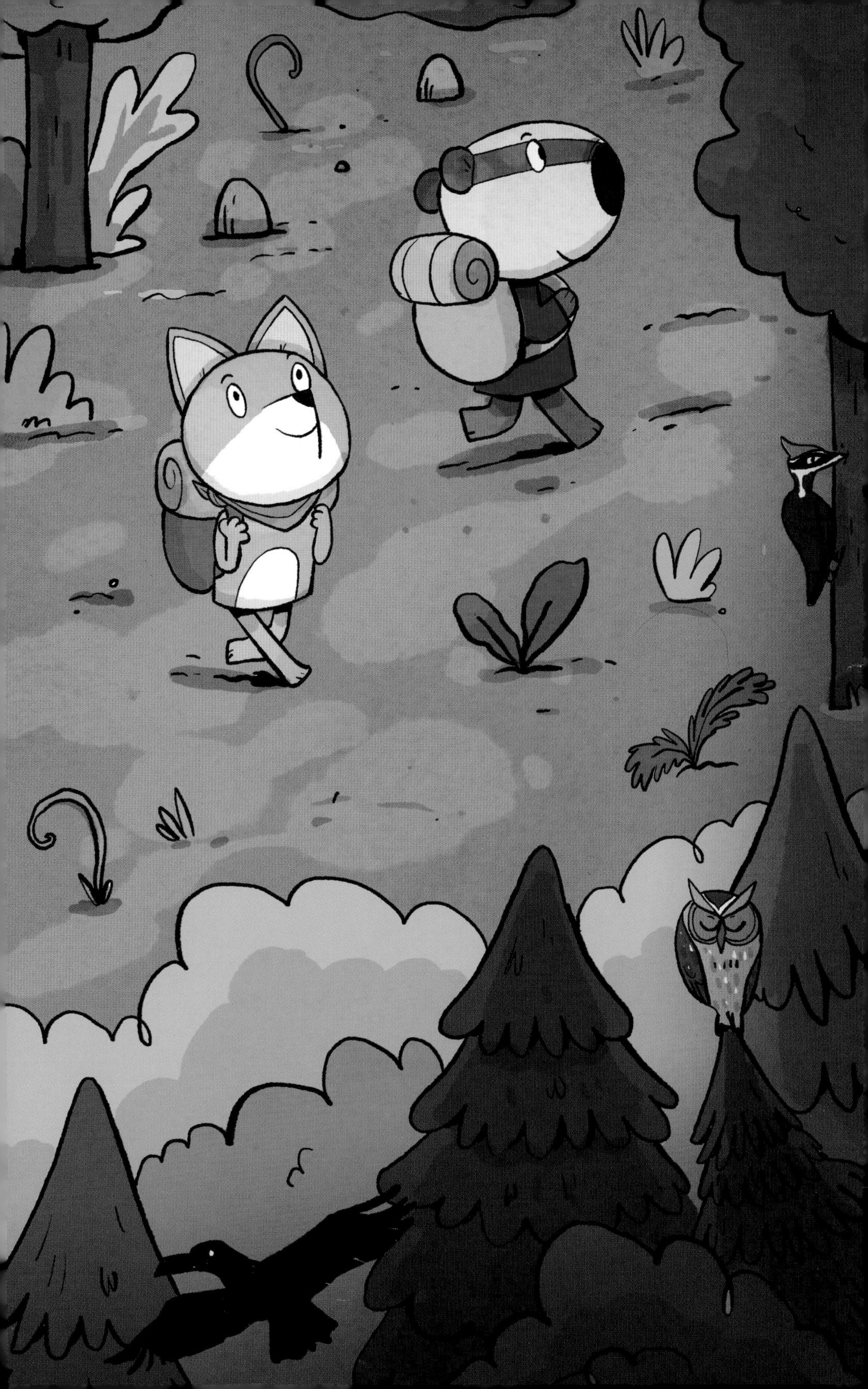

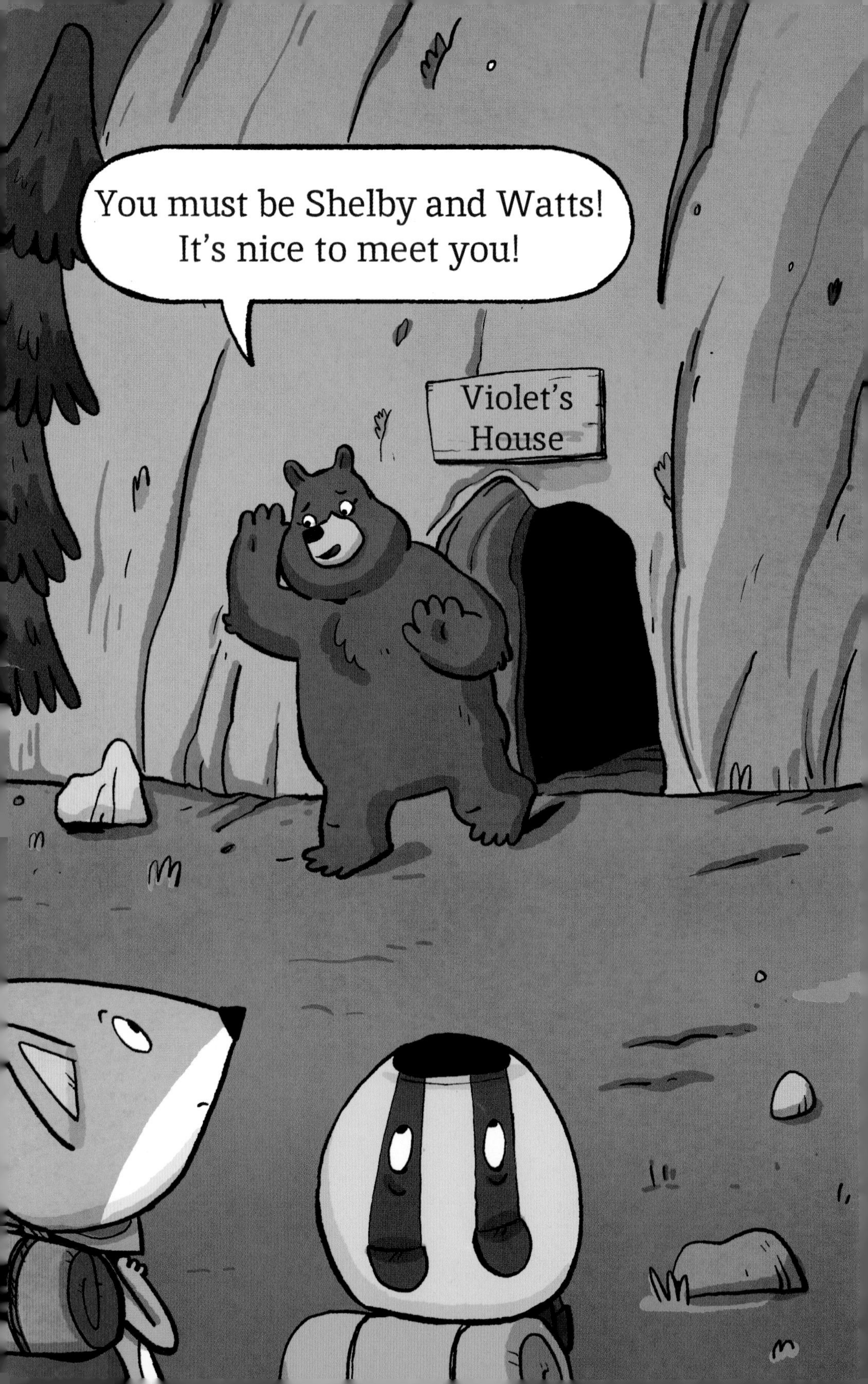
You must be Shelby and Watts! It's nice to meet you!
Violet's House

Violet

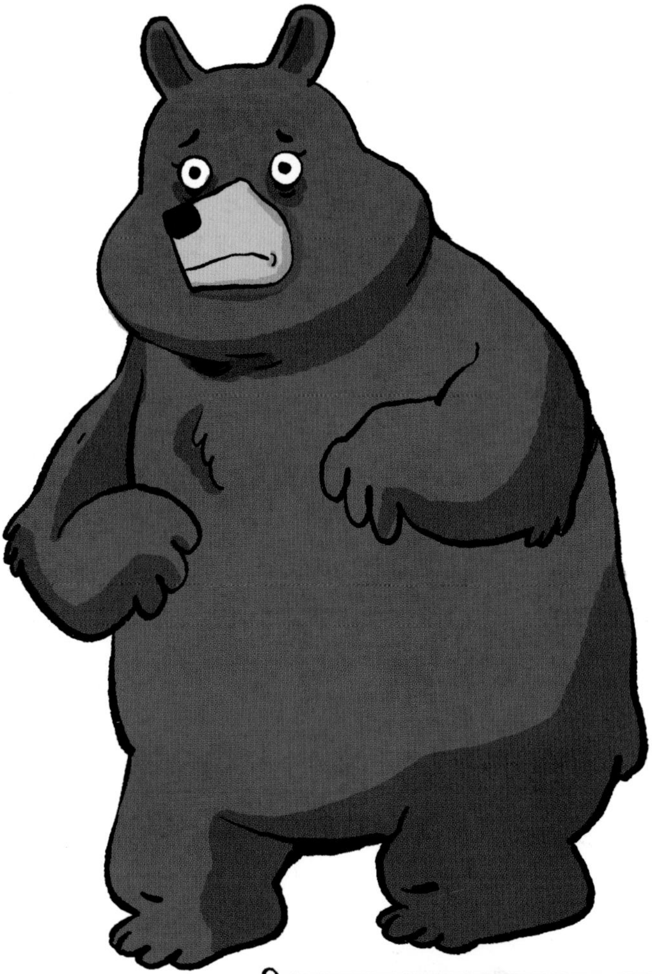

and Theodore

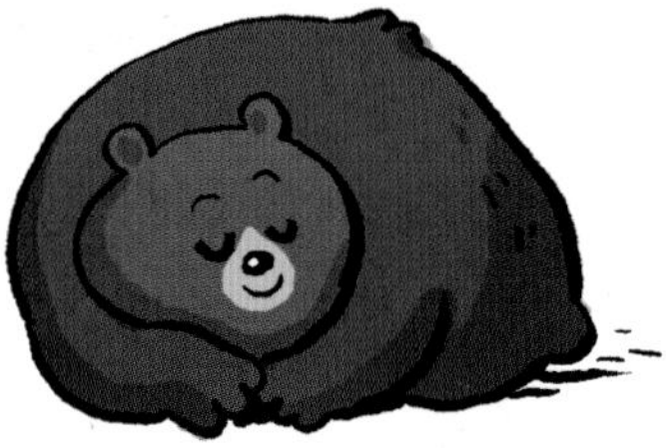

black bear

current mood:
tired, *very* tired
favorite snack: berries

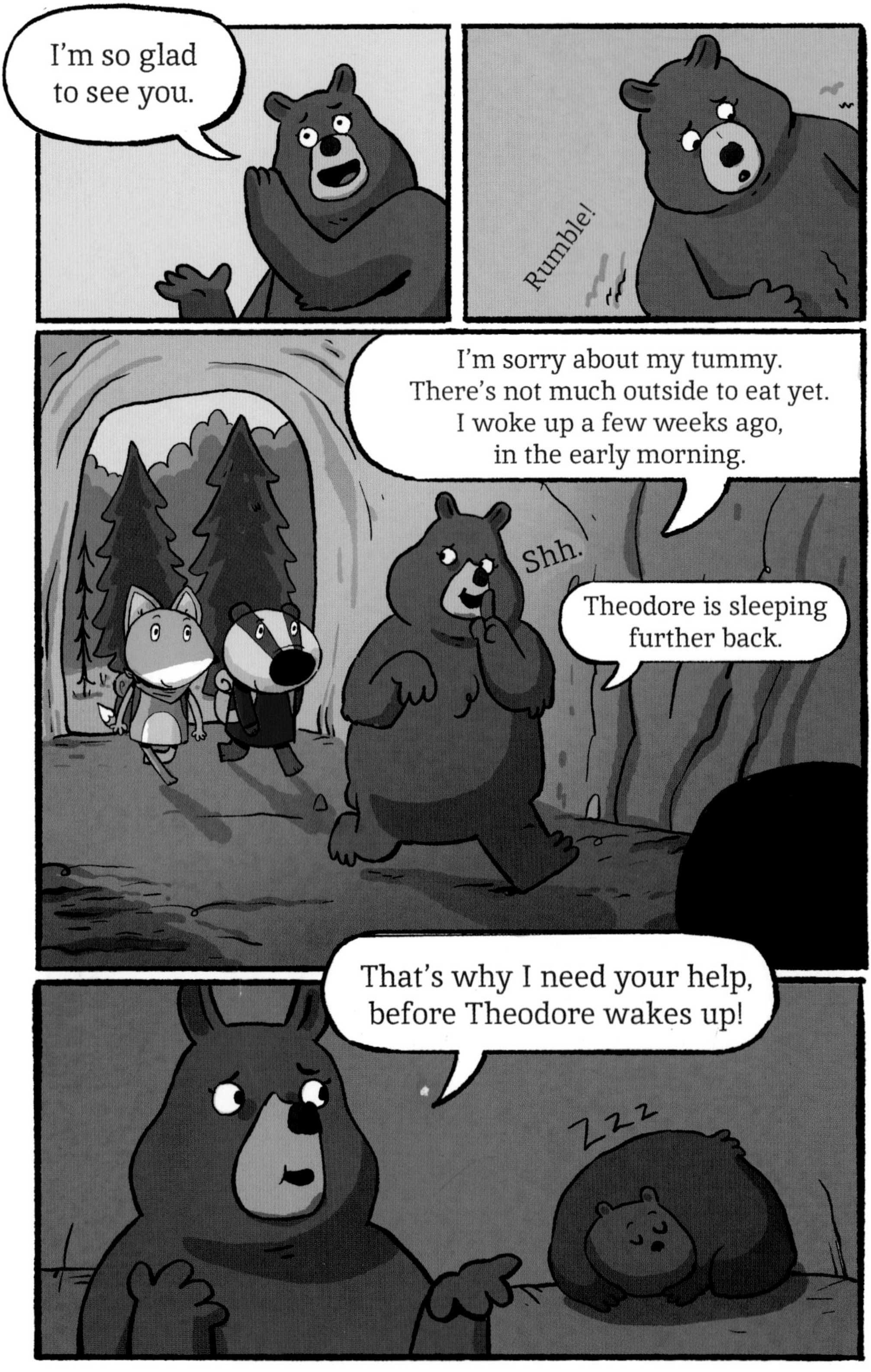
I'm so glad to see you.
Rumble!
I'm sorry about my tummy. There's not much outside to eat yet. I woke up a few weeks ago, in the early morning.
Shh.
Theodore is sleeping further back.
That's why I need your help, before Theodore wakes up!
Z Z Z

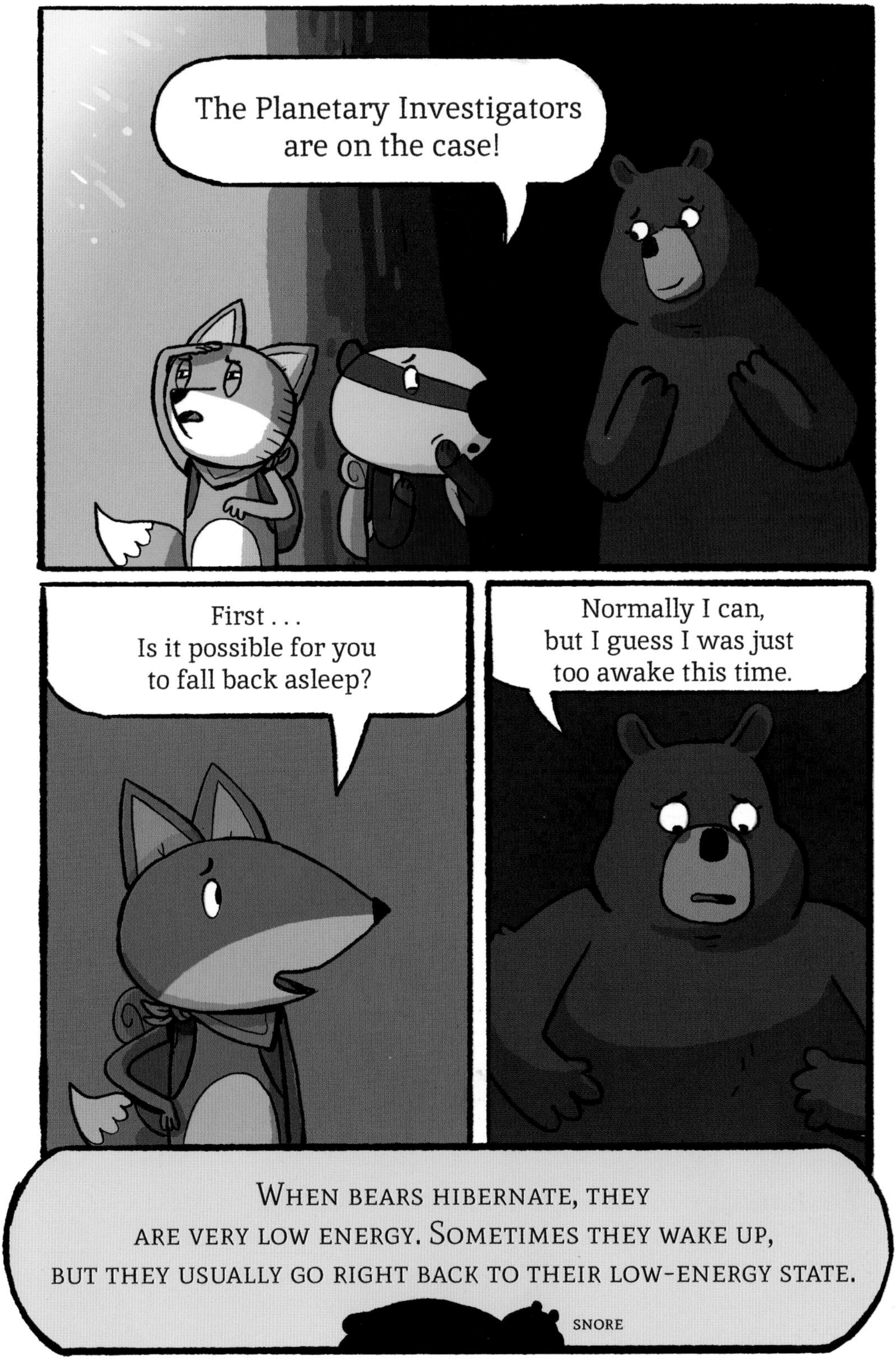
The Planetary Investigators are on the case!
First . . . Is it possible for you to fall back asleep?
Normally I can, but I guess I was just too awake this time.
When bears hibernate, they are very low energy. Sometimes they wake up, but they usually go right back to their low-energy state.
SNORE

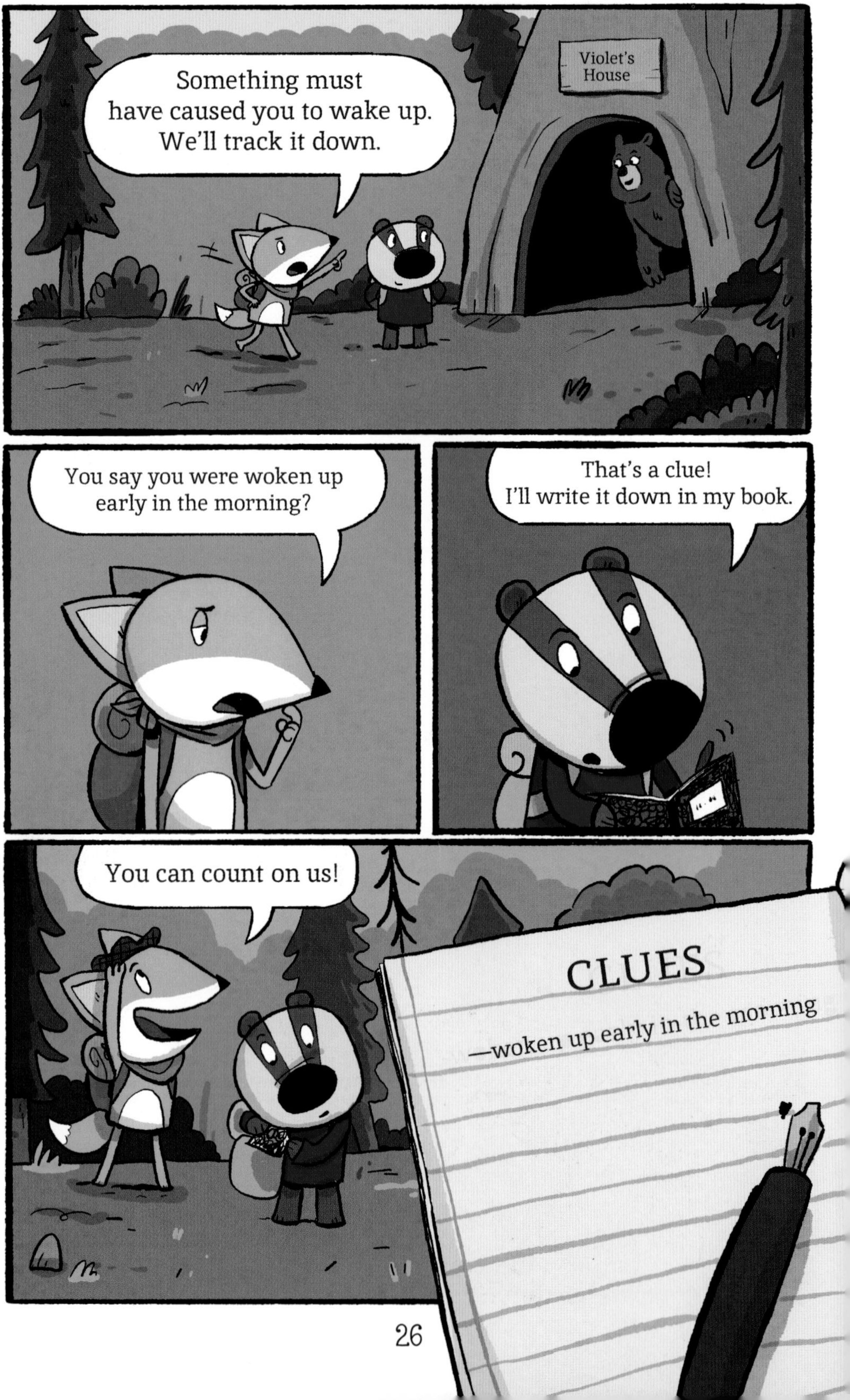
Violet's House
Something must have caused you to wake up. We'll track it down.
You say you were woken up early in the morning?
That's a clue! I'll write it down in my book.
You can count on us!
CLUES
—woken up early in the morning

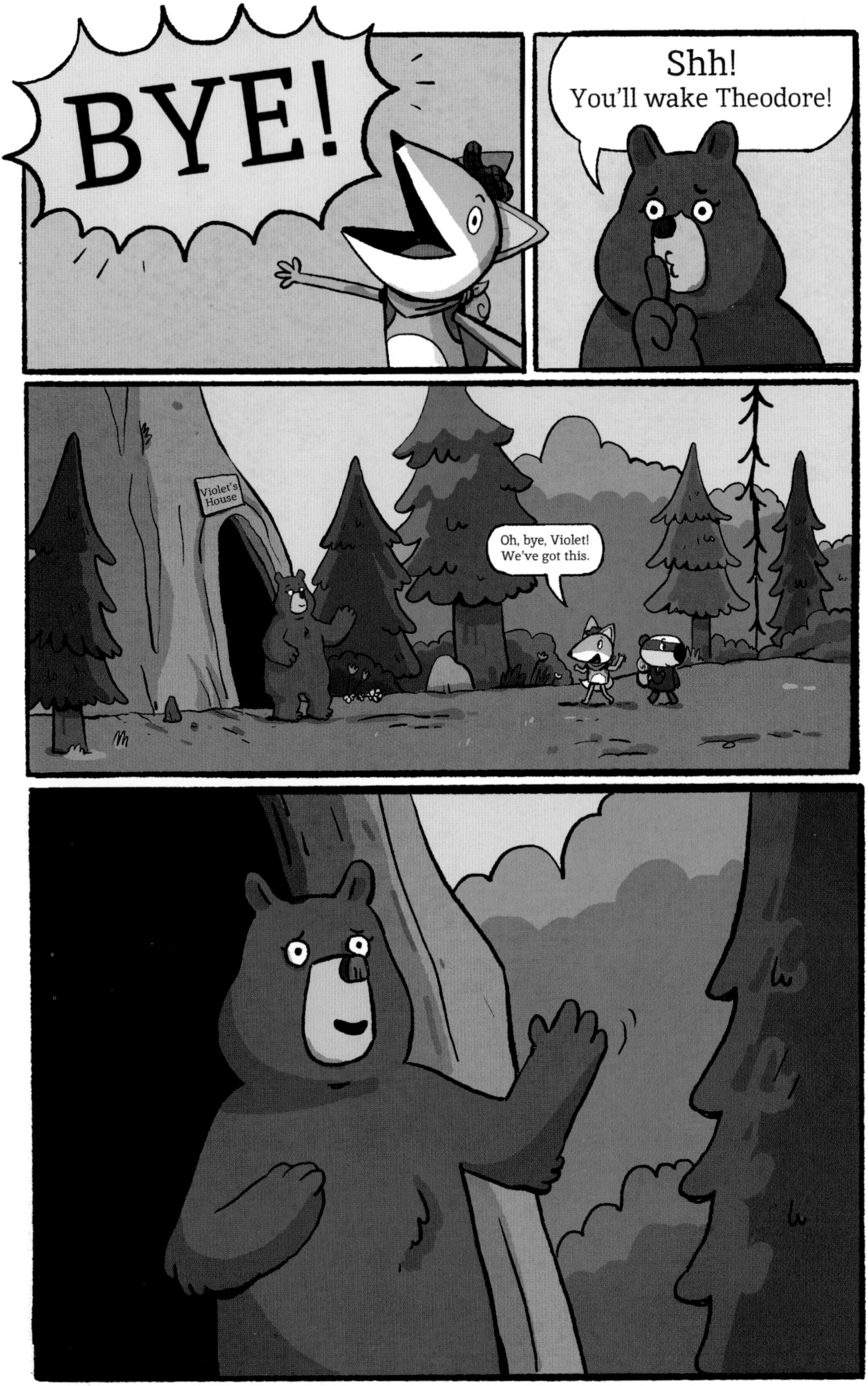
BYE!
Shh!
You'll wake Theodore!
Violet's House
Oh, bye, Violet!
We've got this.

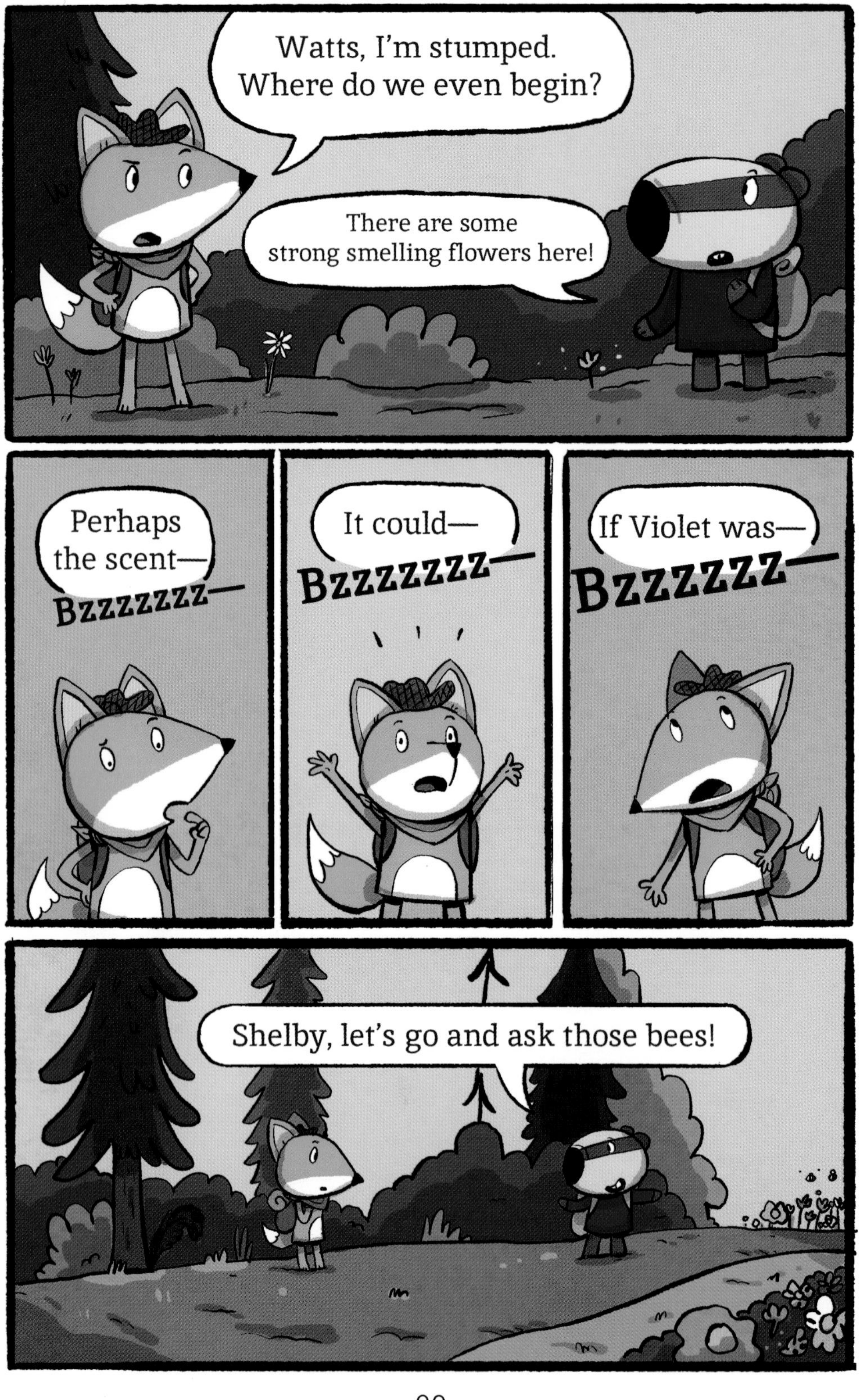
Watts, I'm stumped.
Where do we even begin?
There are some
strong smelling flowers here!
Perhaps
the scent—
Bzzzzzzz—
It could—
Bzzzzzzz—
If Violet was—
Bzzzzzz—
Shelby, let's go and ask those bees!

CHAPTER 3

The flower patch . . .

Bees

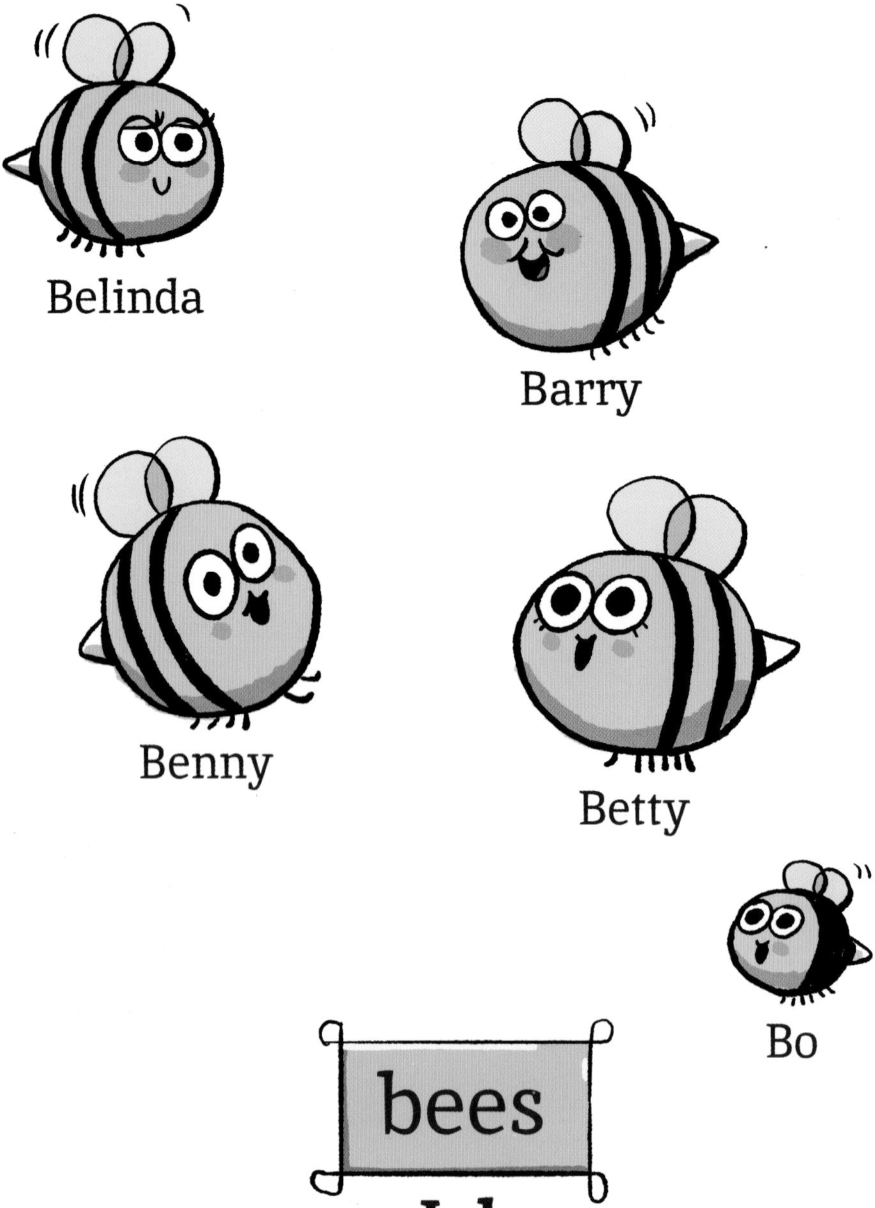
Belinda
Barry
Benny
Betty
Bo
bees

Job:
Pollinating & Bee Stuff
favorite snack: flower pollen

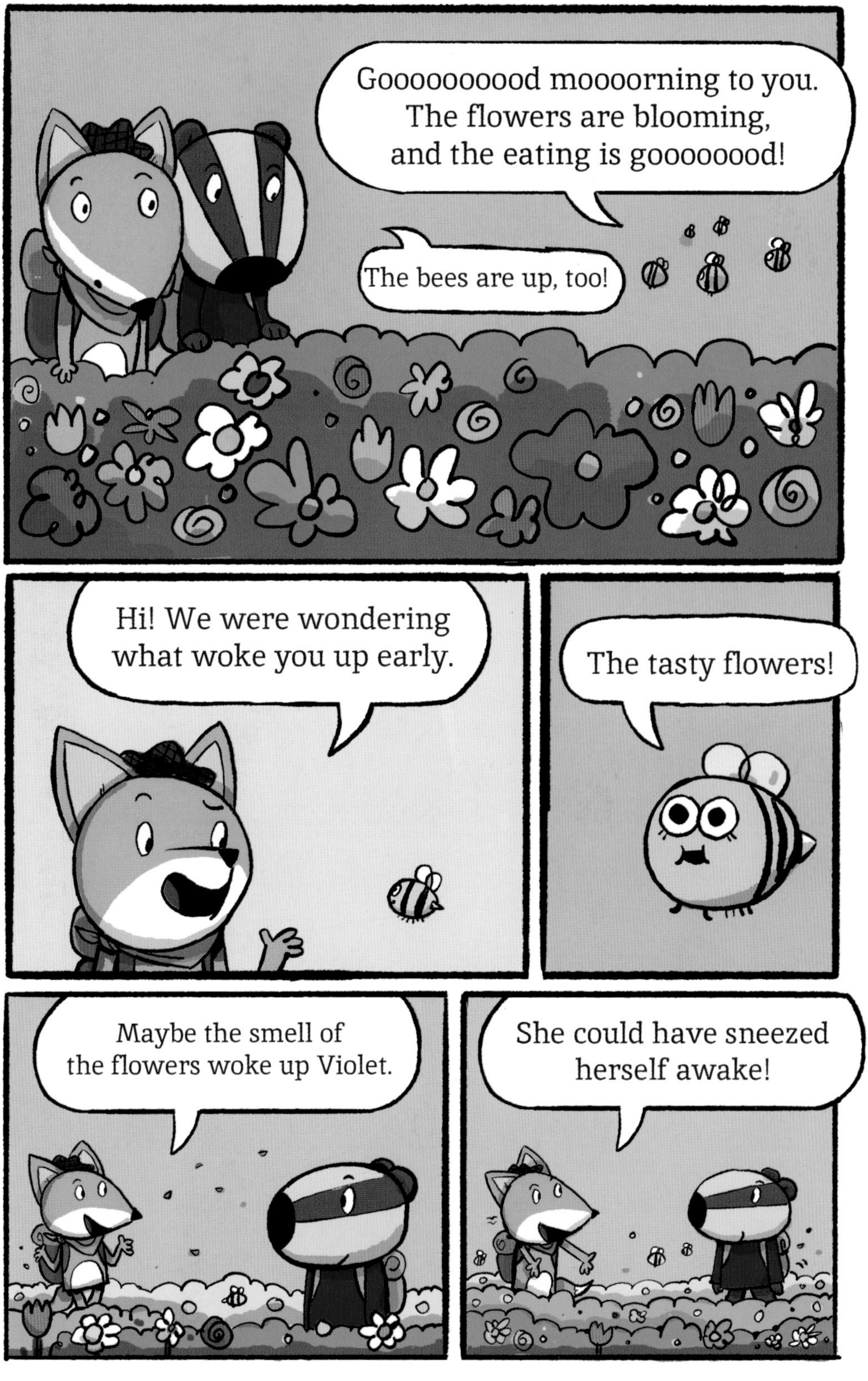
Gooooooooood moooorning to you. The flowers are blooming, and the eating is gooooooood!
The bees are up, too!
Hi! We were wondering what woke you up early.
The tasty flowers!
Maybe the smell of the flowers woke up Violet.
She could have sneezed herself awake!

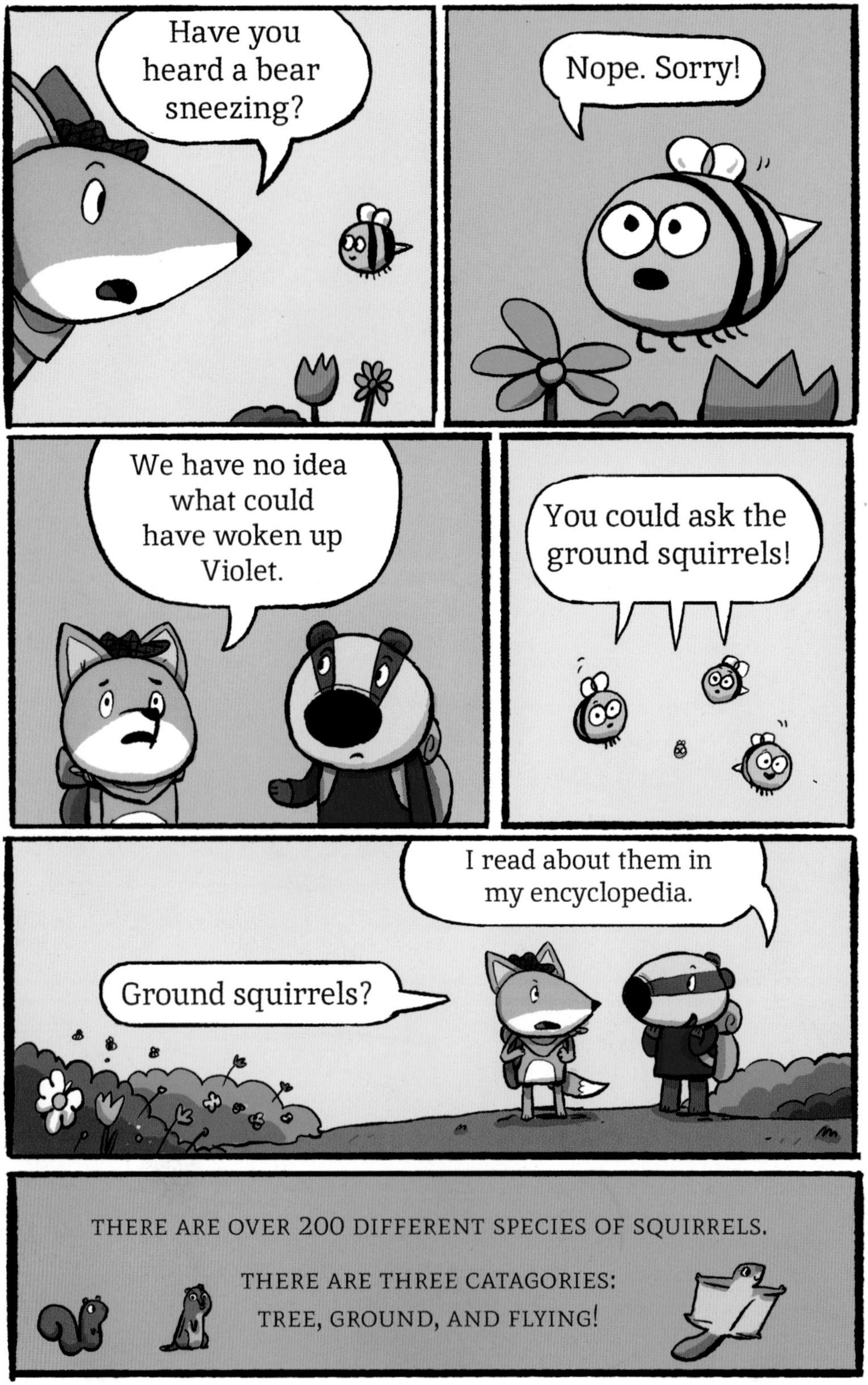
Have you heard a bear sneezing?
Nope. Sorry!
We have no idea what could have woken up Violet.
You could ask the ground squirrels!
I read about them in my encyclopedia.
Ground squirrels?
THERE ARE OVER 200 DIFFERENT SPECIES OF SQUIRRELS.
THERE ARE THREE CATAGORIES:
TREE, GROUND, AND FLYING!

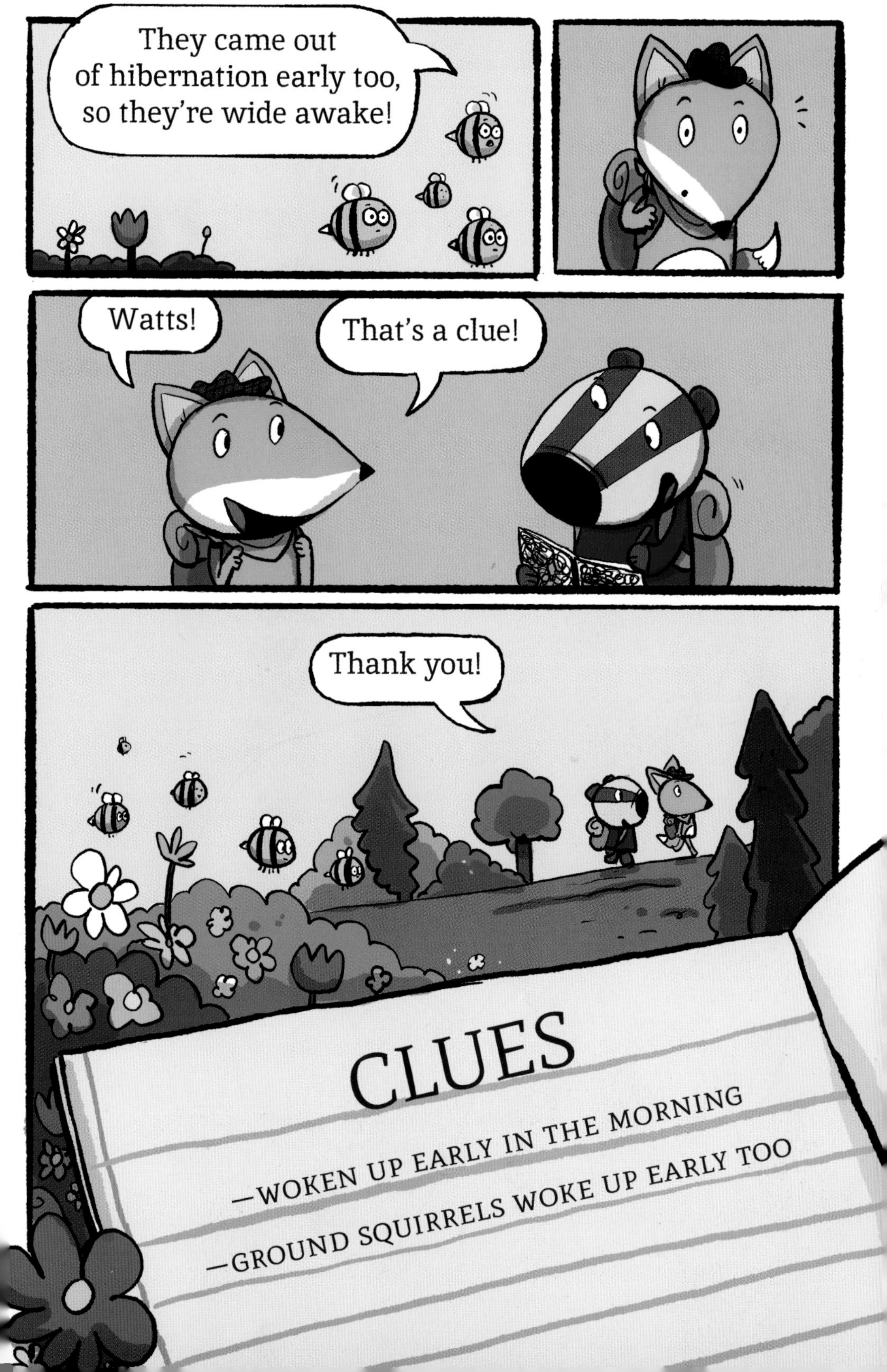
They came out of hibernation early too, so they're wide awake!
Watts!
That's a clue!
Thank you!
CLUES
—WOKEN UP EARLY IN THE MORNING
—GROUND SQUIRRELS WOKE UP EARLY TOO

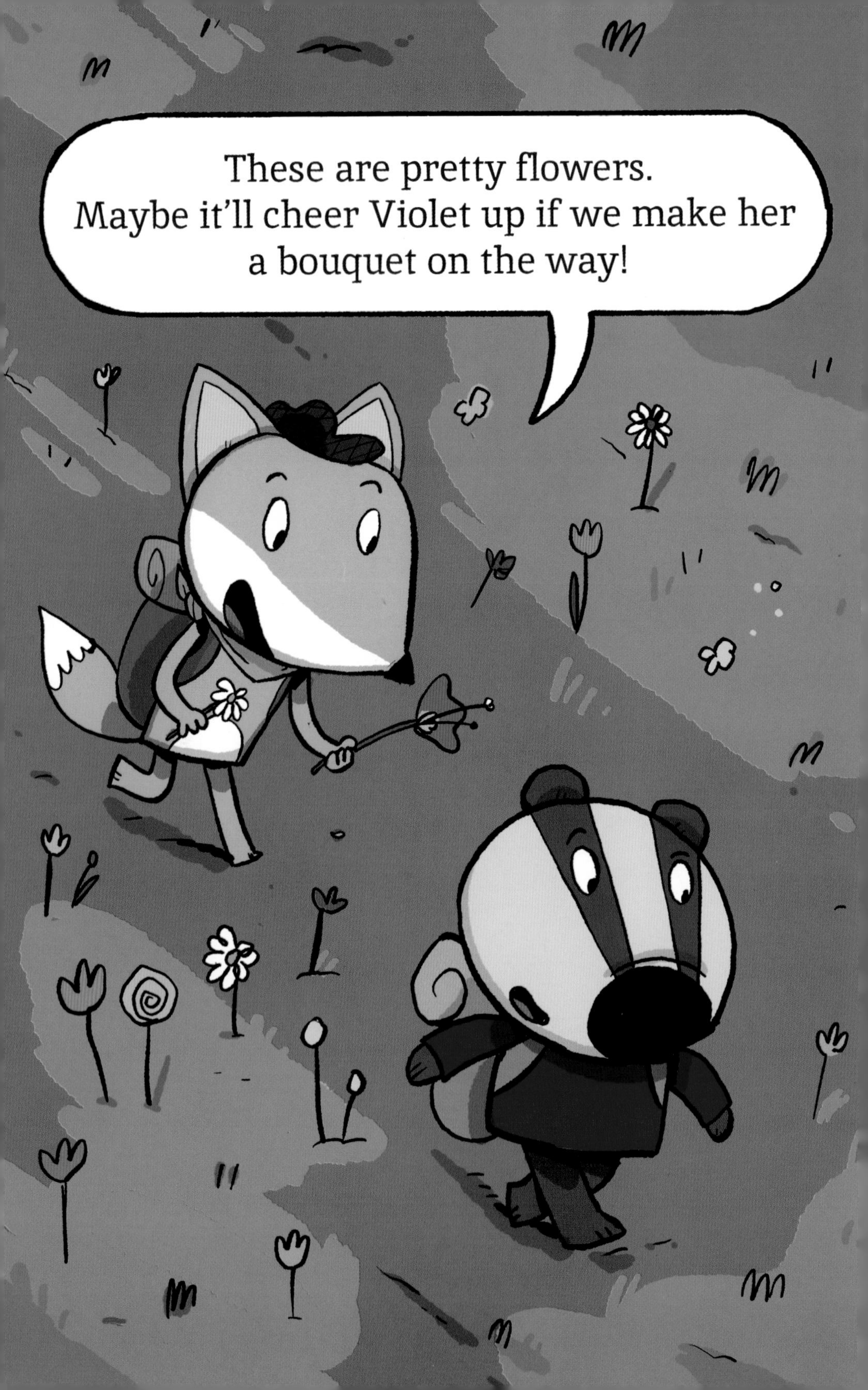
These are pretty flowers. Maybe it'll cheer Violet up if we make her a bouquet on the way!

CHAPTER 4

Near the oak trees . . .

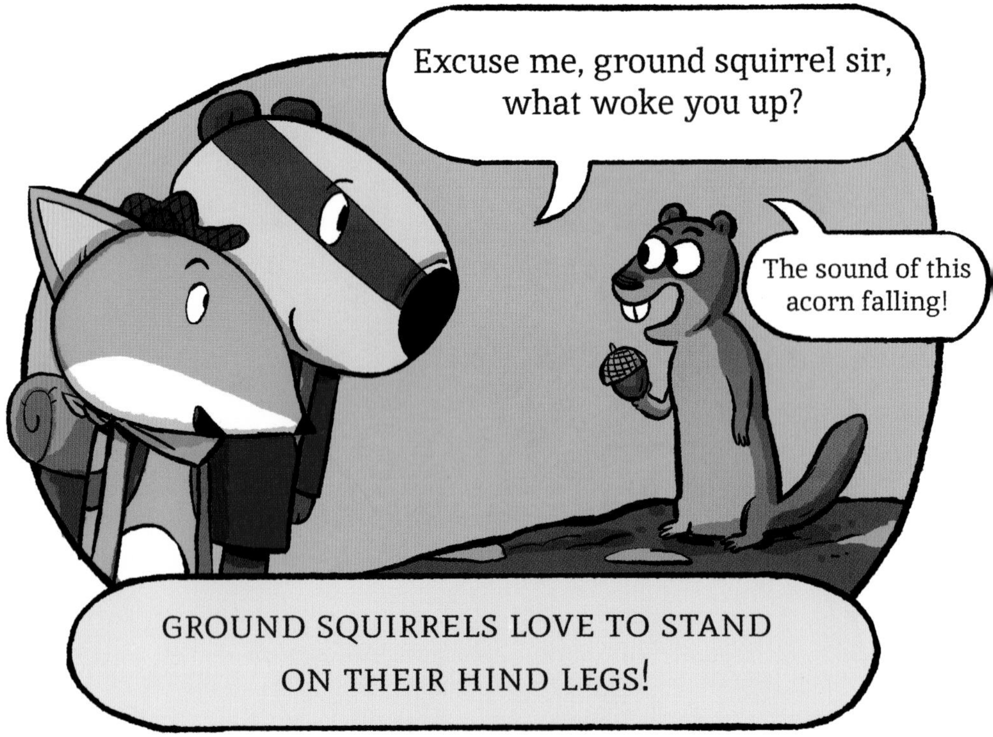
Excuse me, ground squirrel sir, what woke you up?
The sound of this acorn falling!
GROUND SQUIRRELS LOVE TO STAND ON THEIR HIND LEGS!

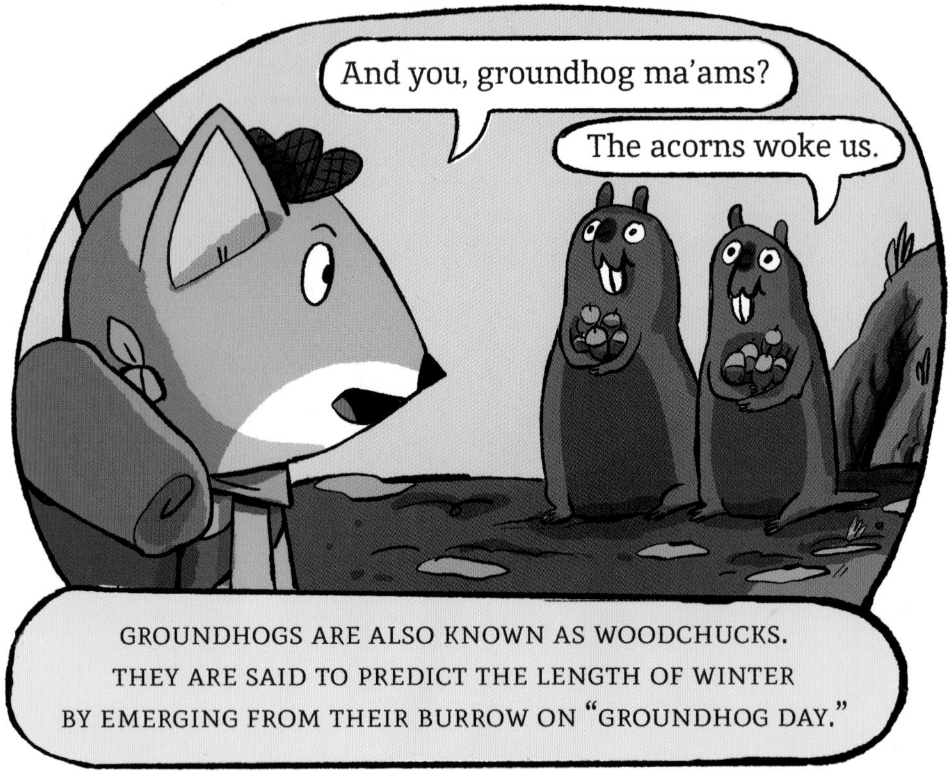
And you, groundhog ma'ams?
The acorns woke us.
GROUNDHOGS ARE ALSO KNOWN AS WOODCHUCKS. THEY ARE SAID TO PREDICT THE LENGTH OF WINTER BY EMERGING FROM THEIR BURROW ON "GROUNDHOG DAY."

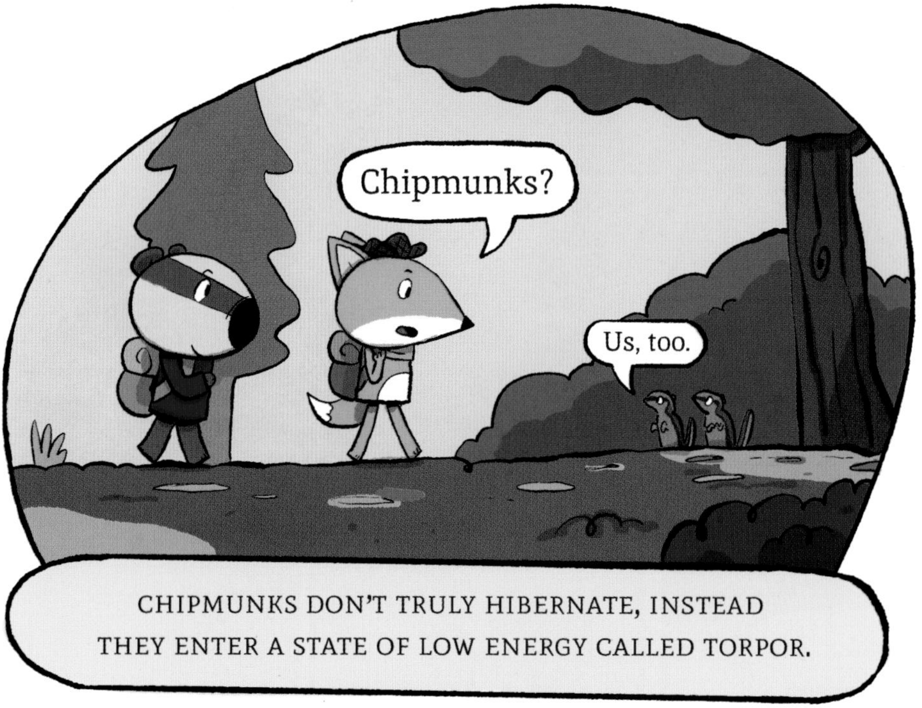
Chipmunks?
Us, too.
CHIPMUNKS DON'T TRULY HIBERNATE, INSTEAD THEY ENTER A STATE OF LOW ENERGY CALLED TORPOR.

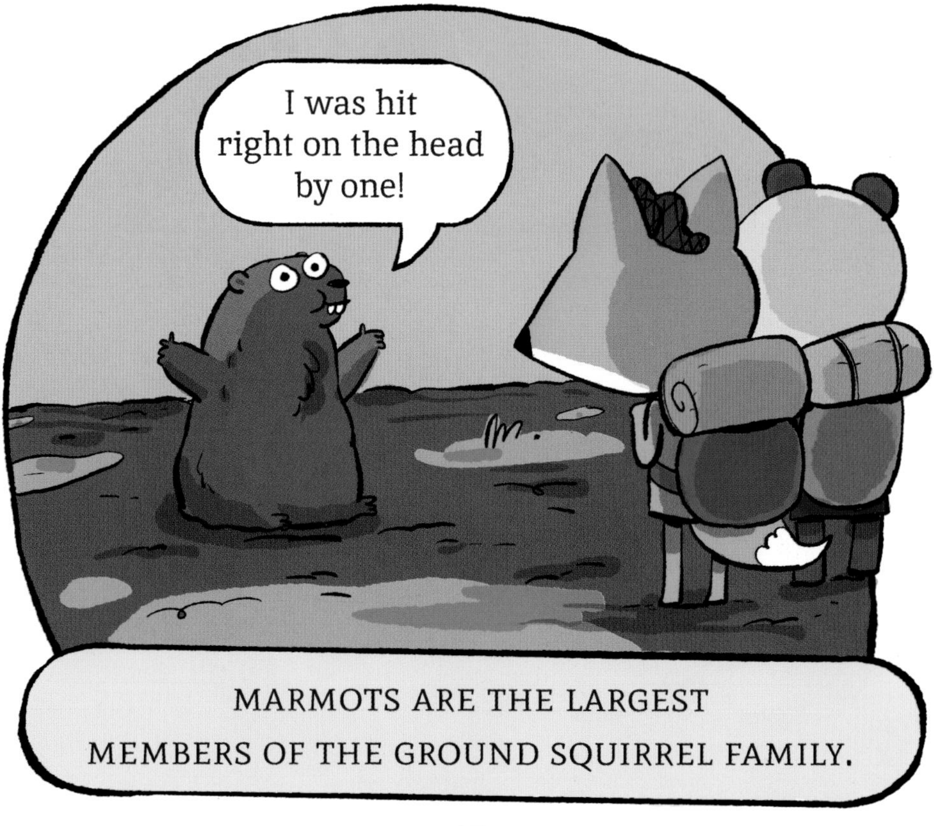
I was hit right on the head by one!
MARMOTS ARE THE LARGEST MEMBERS OF THE GROUND SQUIRREL FAMILY.

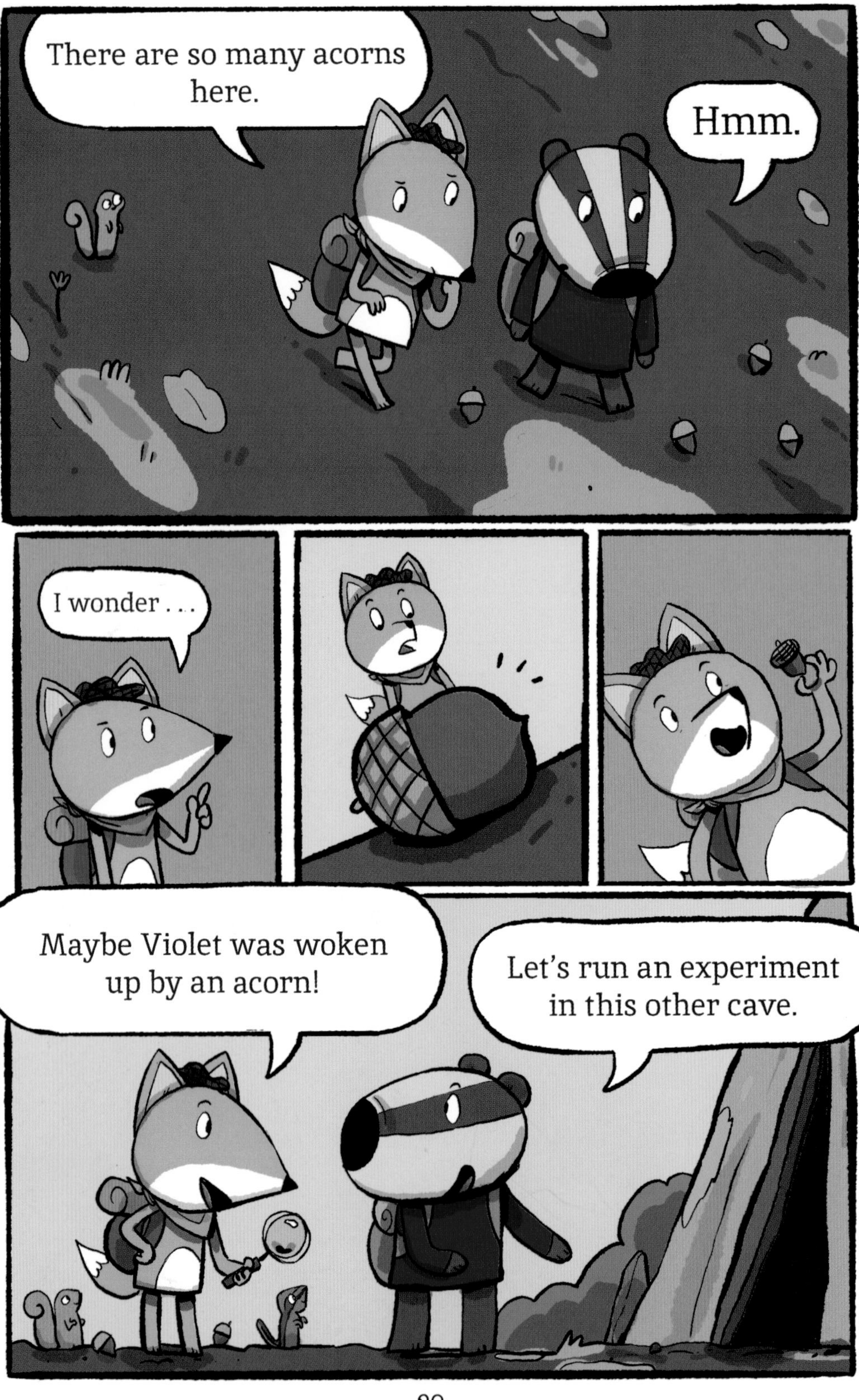
There are so many acorns here.
Hmm.
I wonder . . .
Maybe Violet was woken up by an acorn!
Let's run an experiment in this other cave.

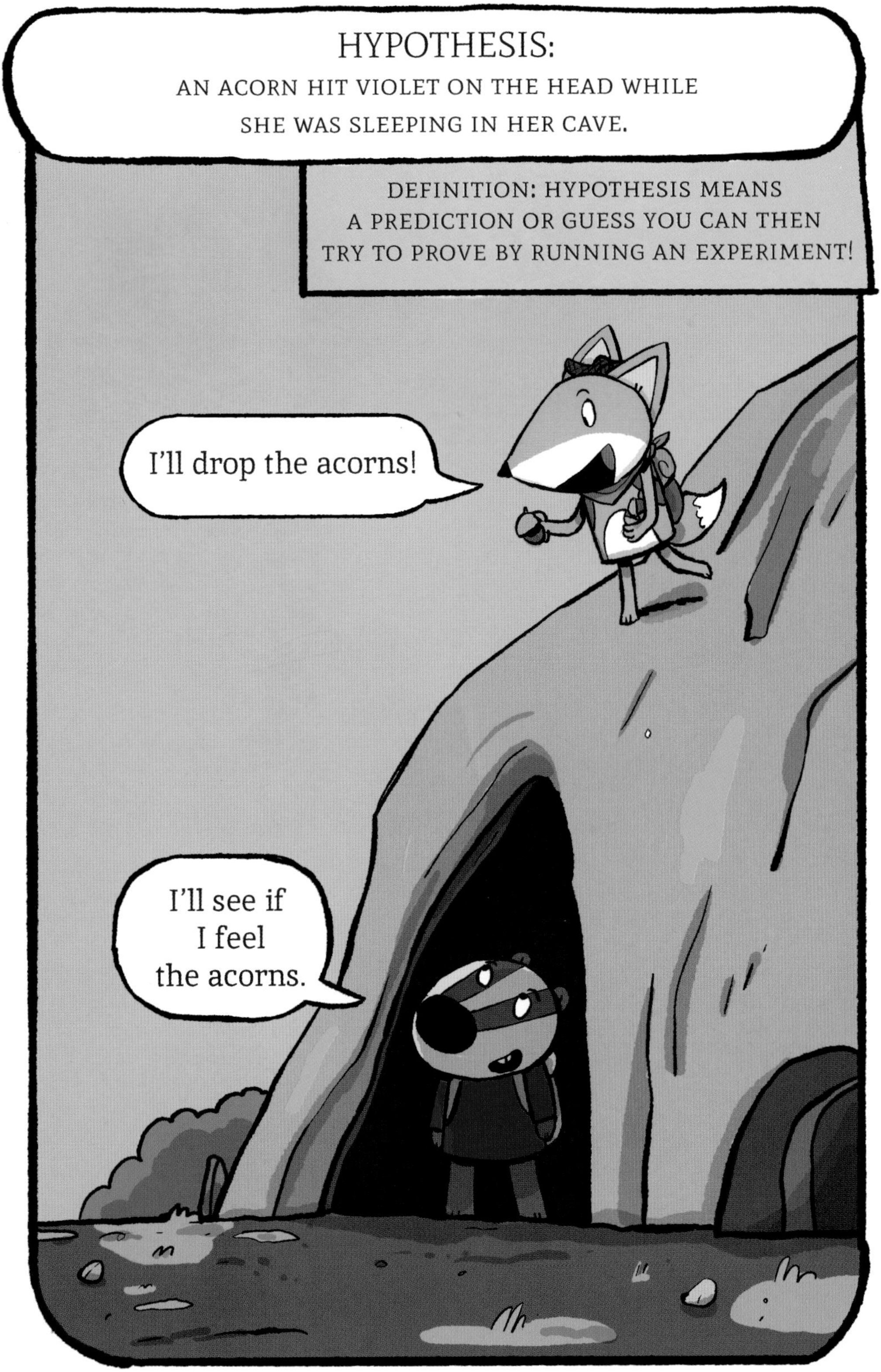
HYPOTHESIS:
AN ACORN HIT VIOLET ON THE HEAD WHILE SHE WAS SLEEPING IN HER CAVE.
DEFINITION: HYPOTHESIS MEANS A PREDICTION OR GUESS YOU CAN THEN TRY TO PROVE BY RUNNING AN EXPERIMENT!
I'll drop the acorns!
I'll see if I feel the acorns.

Acorns
aweigh!

Thud!

Are any acorns
hitting you?

No.

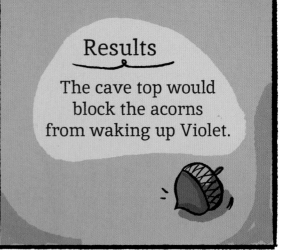

Results

The cave top would
block the acorns
from waking up Violet.

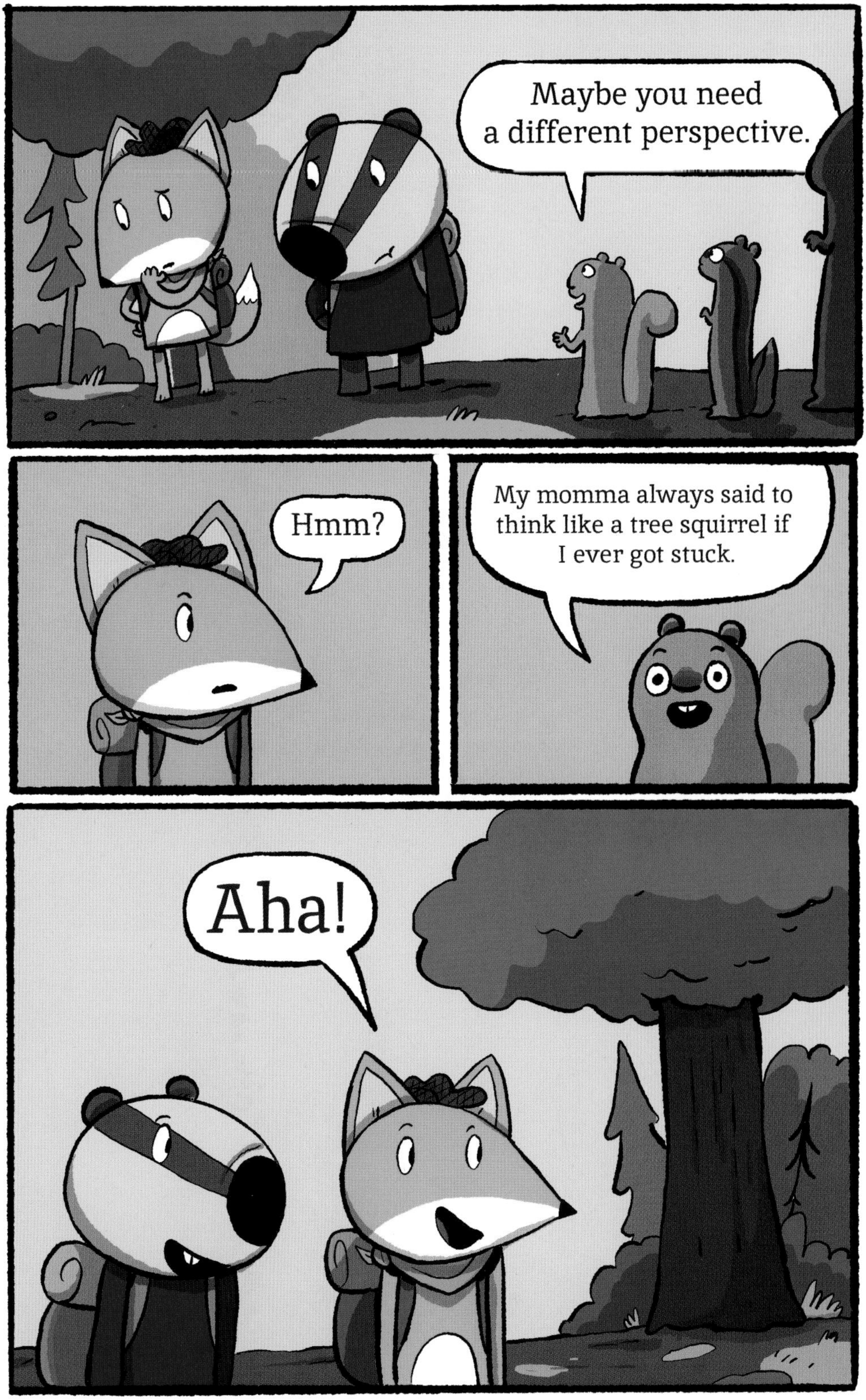
Maybe you need
a different perspective.
Hmm?
My momma always said to
think like a tree squirrel if
I ever got stuck.
Aha!

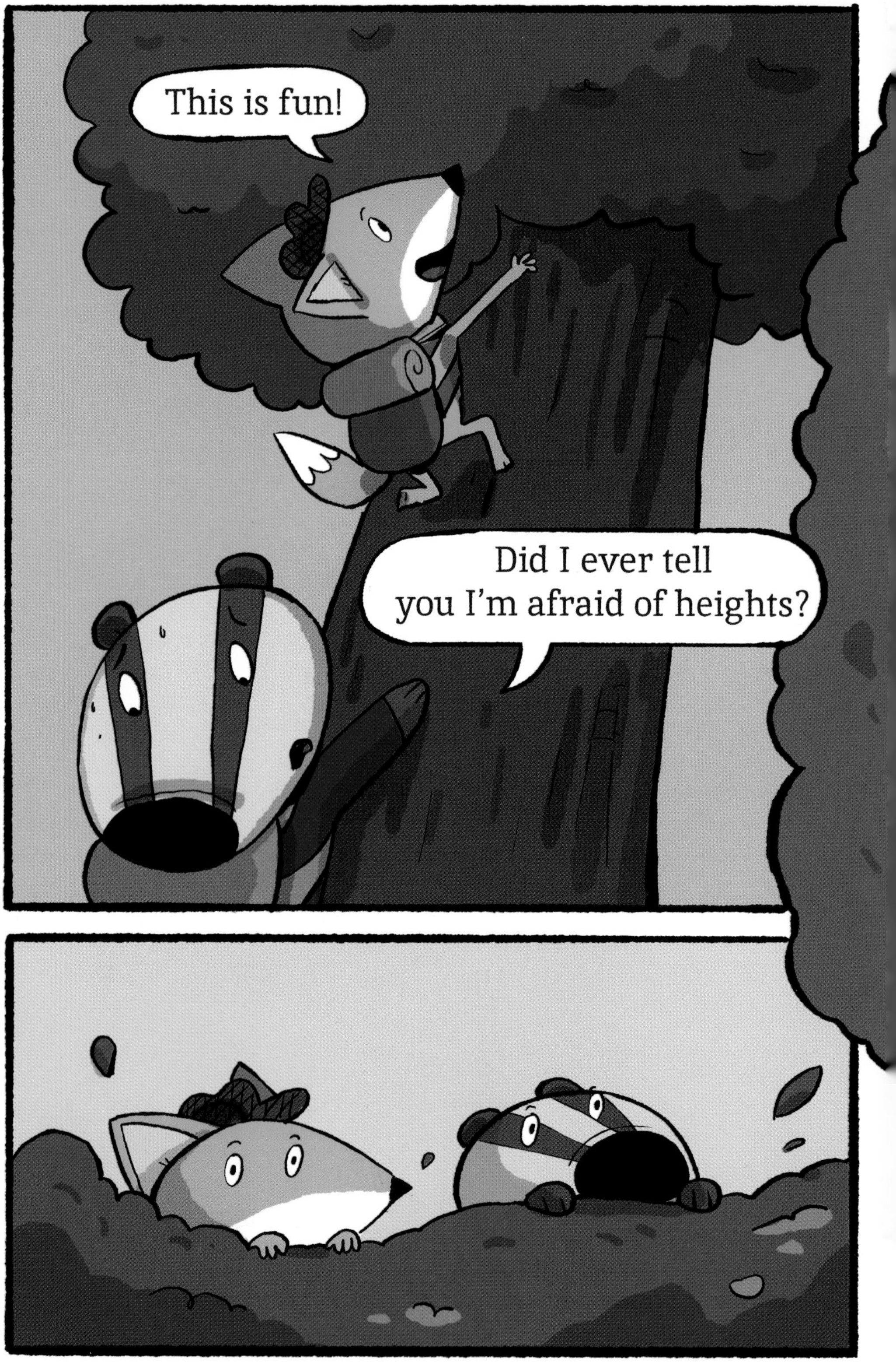
This is fun!
Did I ever tell you I'm afraid of heights?

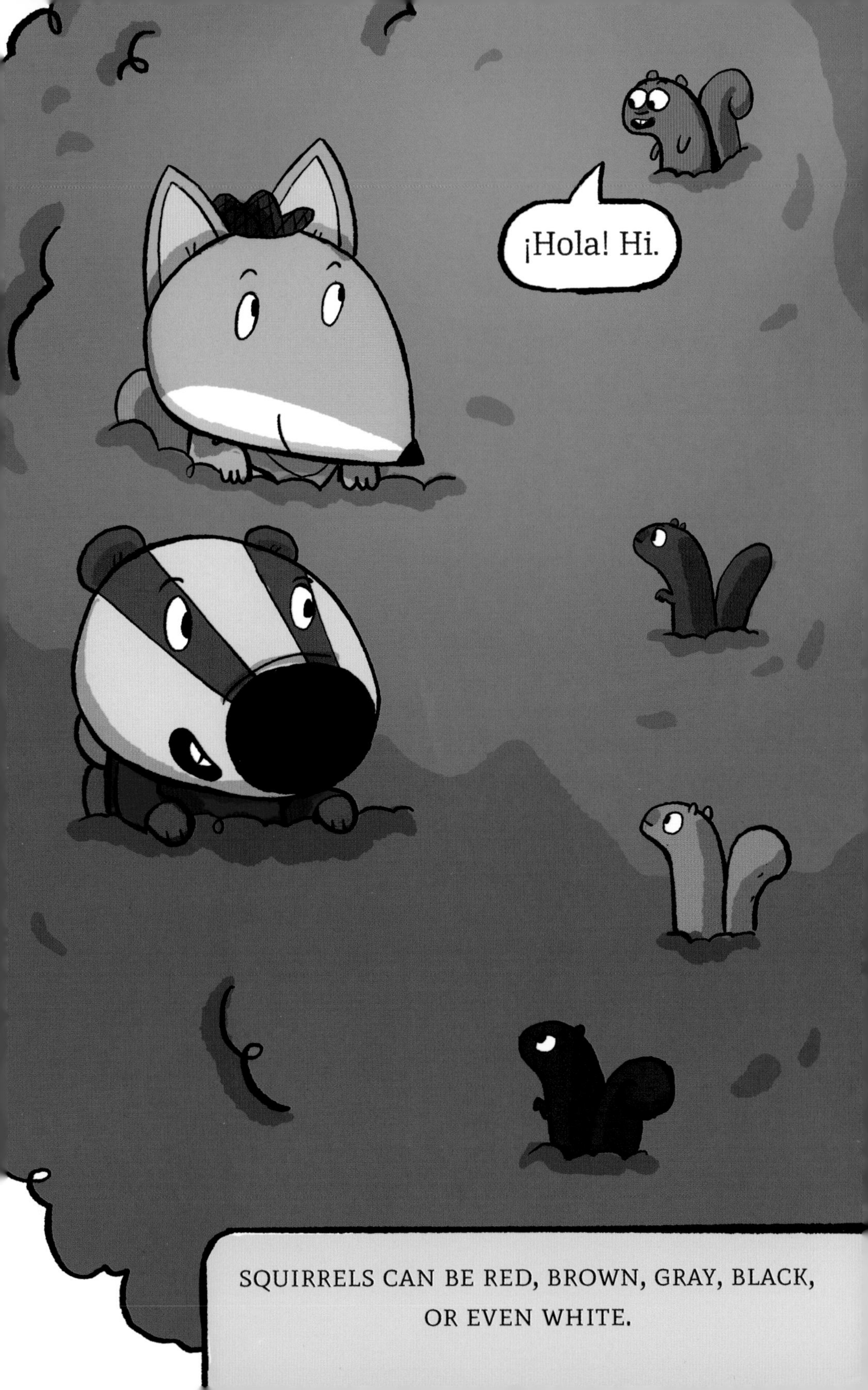
¡Hola! Hi.
SQUIRRELS CAN BE RED, BROWN, GRAY, BLACK, OR EVEN WHITE.

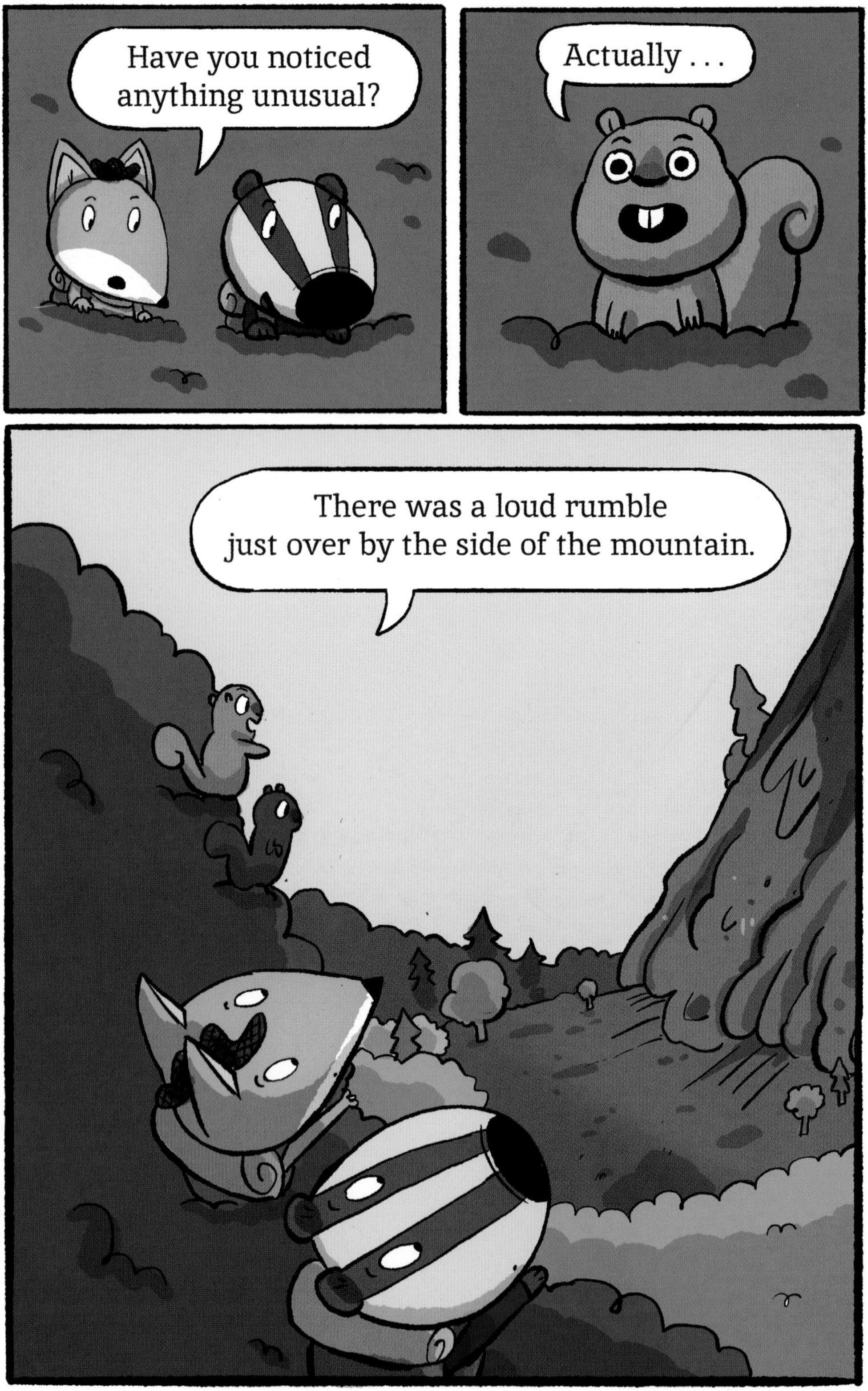
Have you noticed anything unusual?
Actually . . .
There was a loud rumble just over by the side of the mountain.

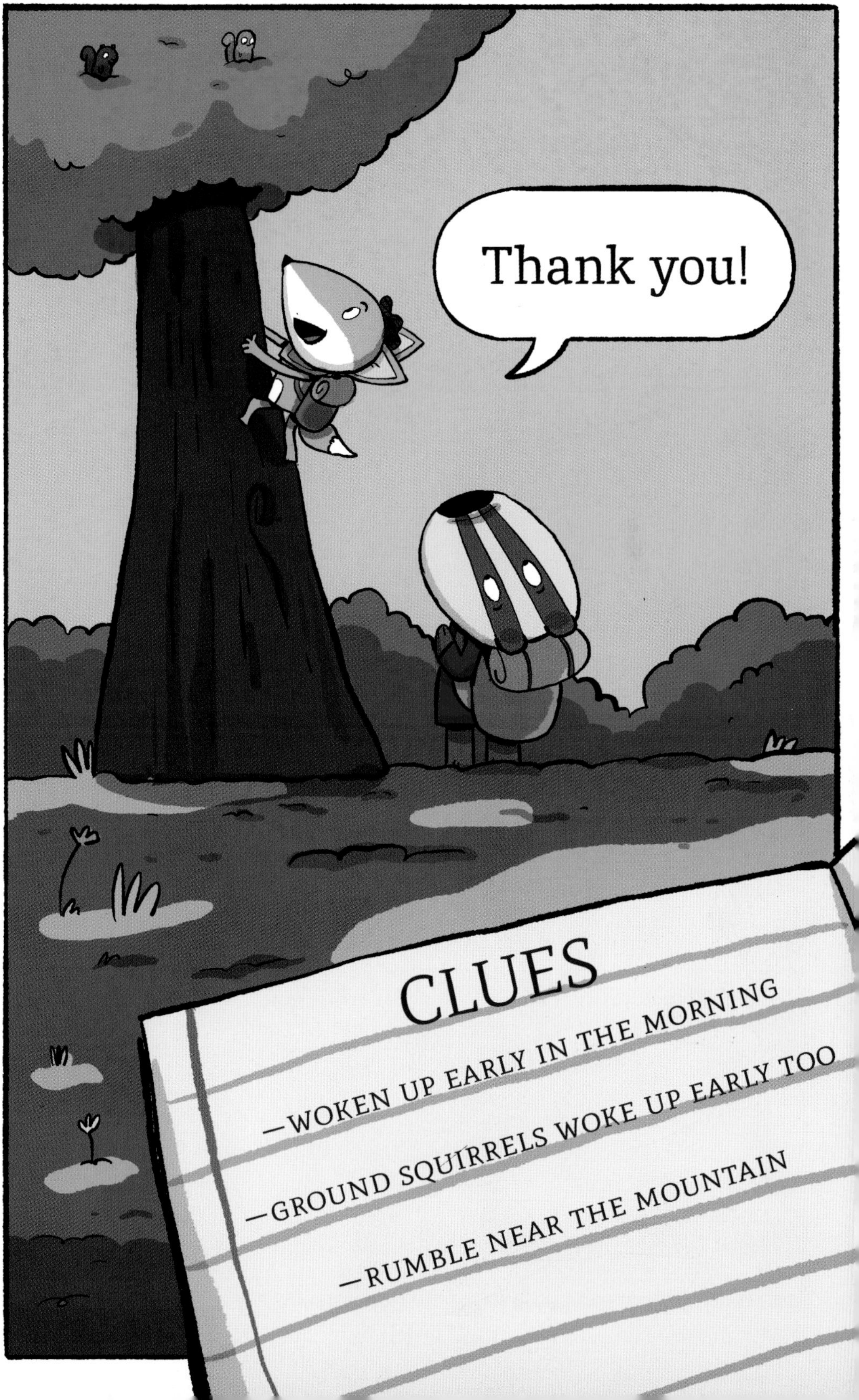
Thank you!
CLUES
—WOKEN UP EARLY IN THE MORNING
—GROUND SQUIRRELS WOKE UP EARLY TOO
—RUMBLE NEAR THE MOUNTAIN

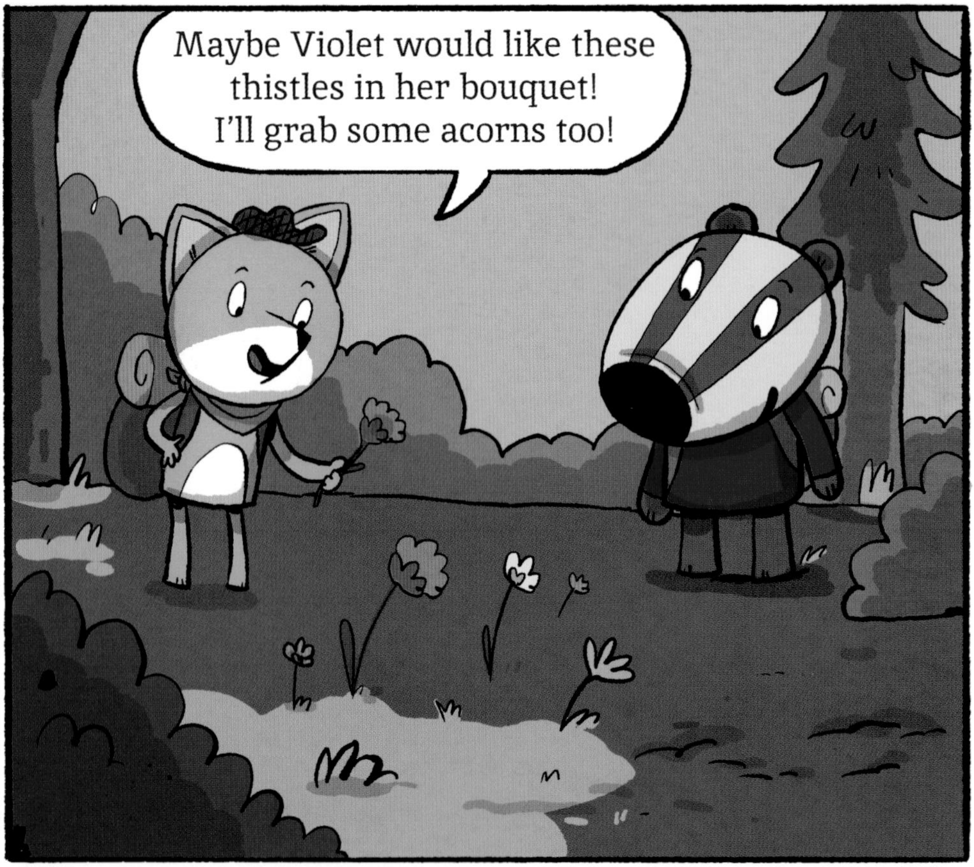
Maybe Violet would like these thistles in her bouquet! I'll grab some acorns too!

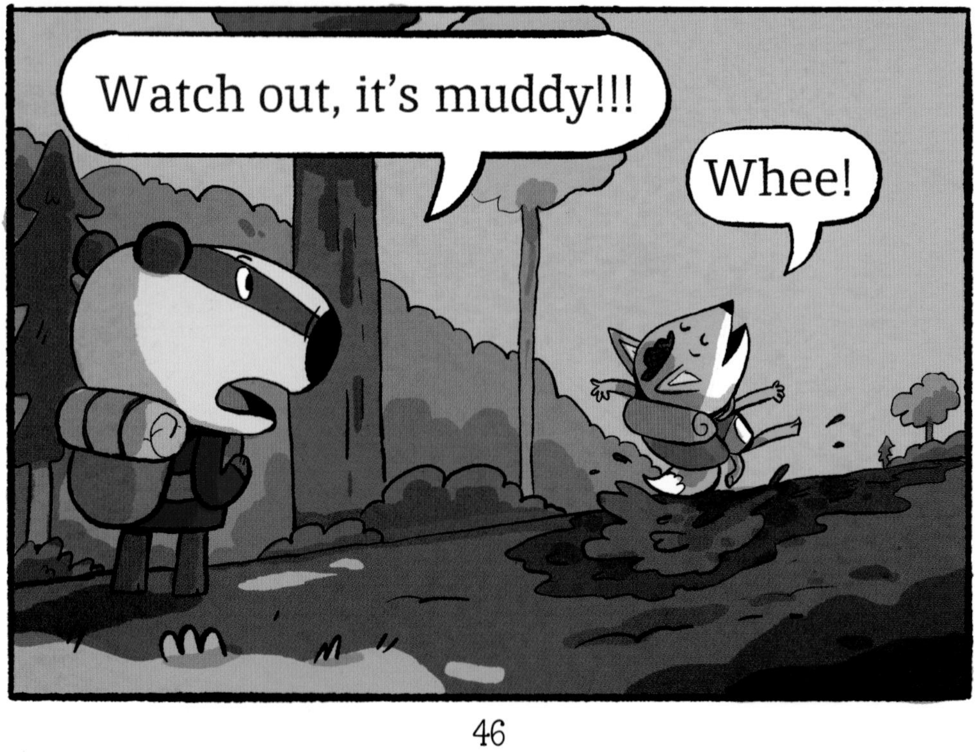
Watch out, it's muddy!!!
Whee!

CHAPTER 5

The side of the mountain . . .

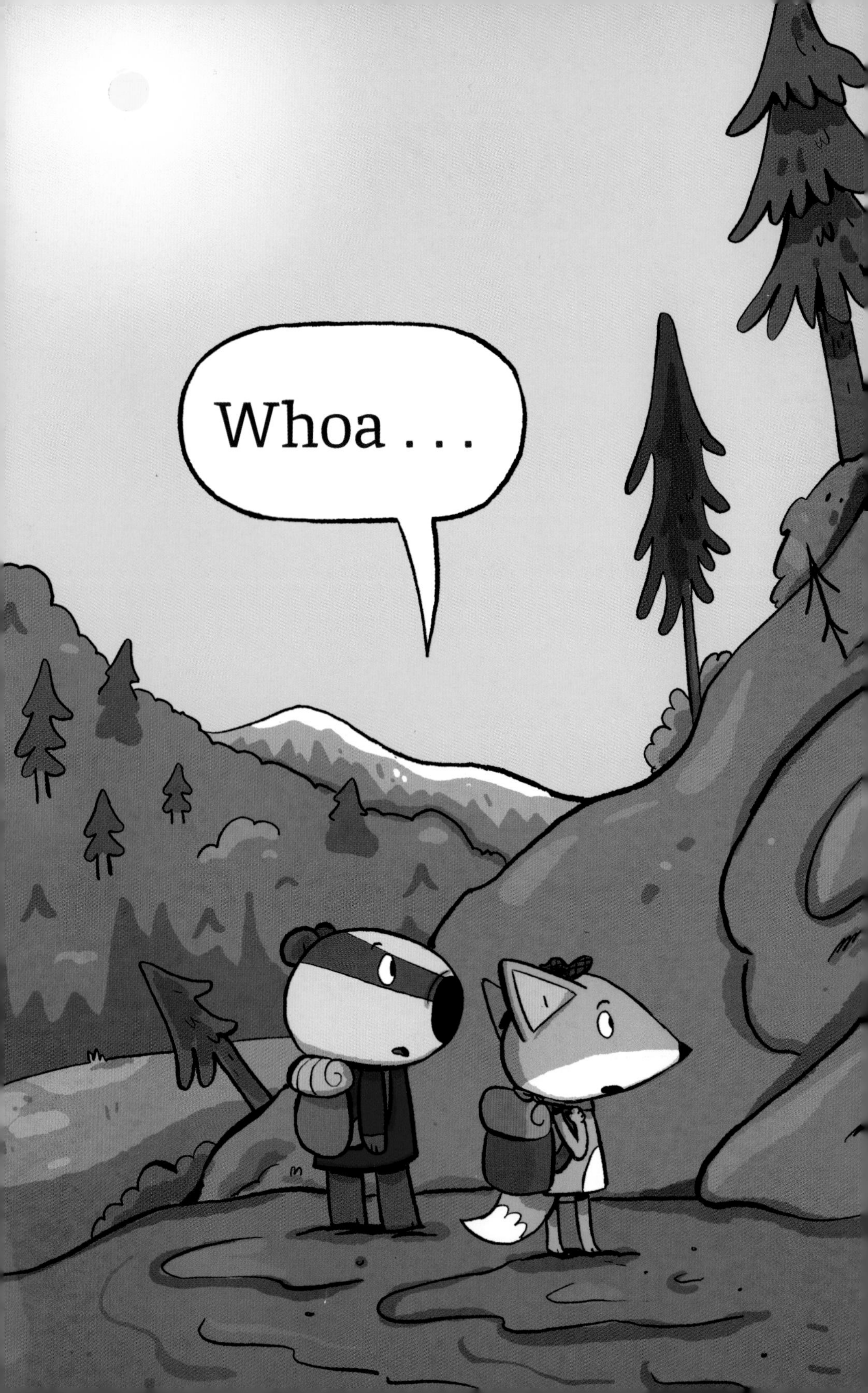
Whoa . . .

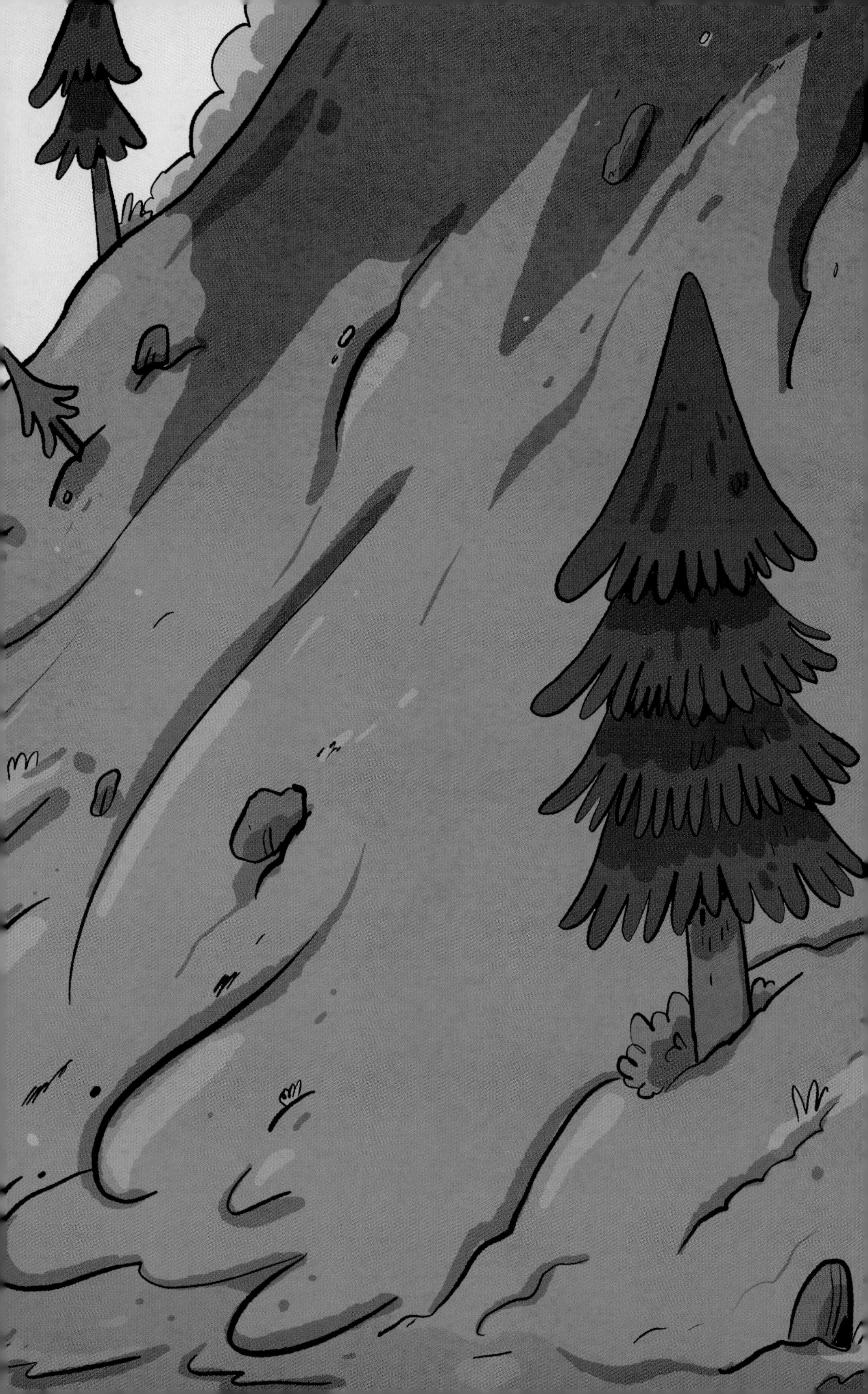

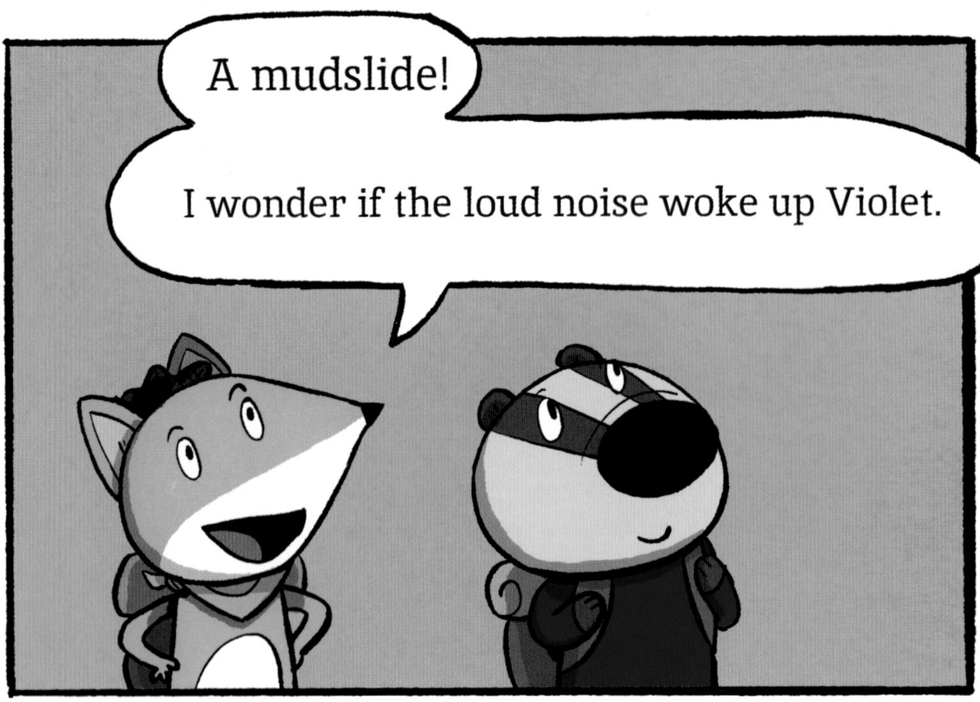
A mudslide!
I wonder if the loud noise woke up Violet.

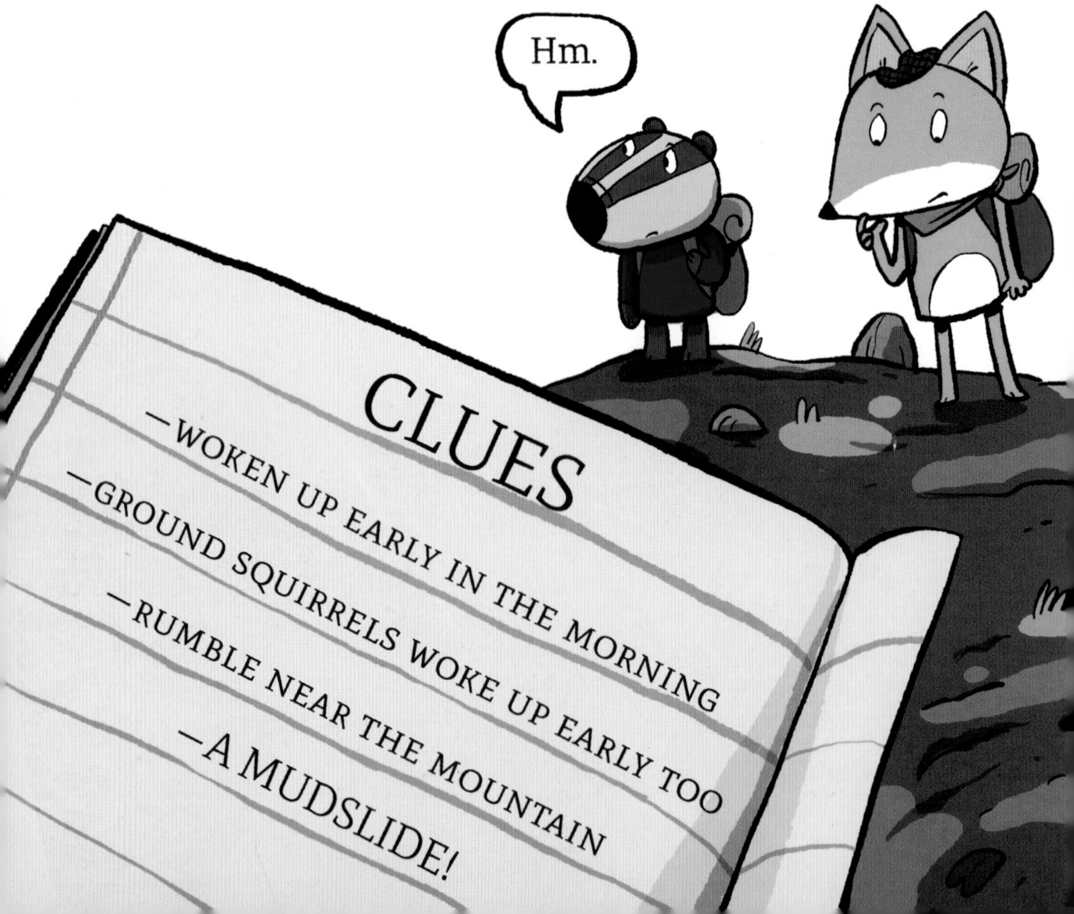
Hm.
CLUES
—WOKEN UP EARLY IN THE MORNING
—GROUND SQUIRRELS WOKE UP EARLY TOO
—RUMBLE NEAR THE MOUNTAIN
—A MUDSLIDE!

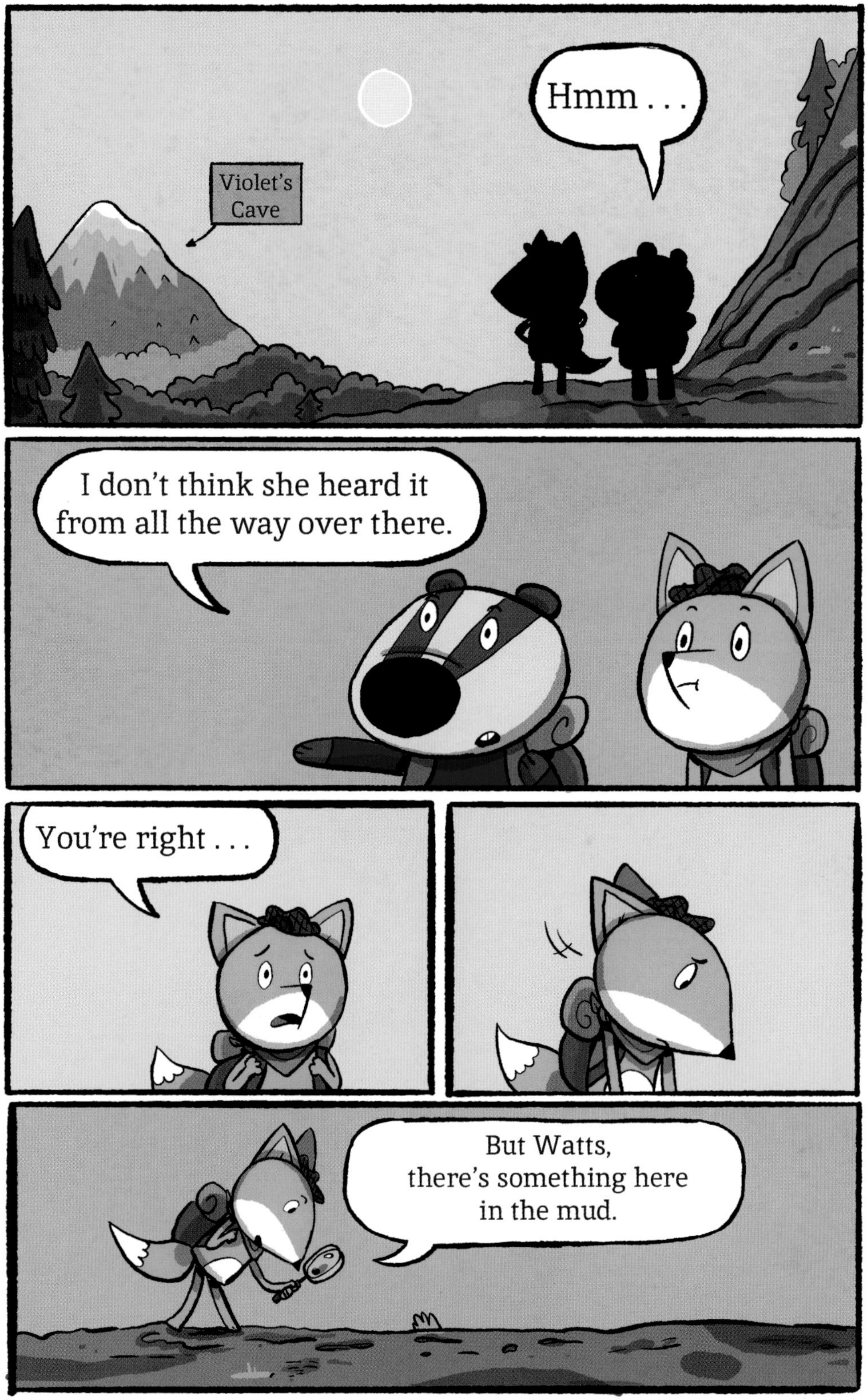
Violet's Cave
Hmm . . .
I don't think she heard it from all the way over there.
You're right . . .
But Watts, there's something here in the mud.

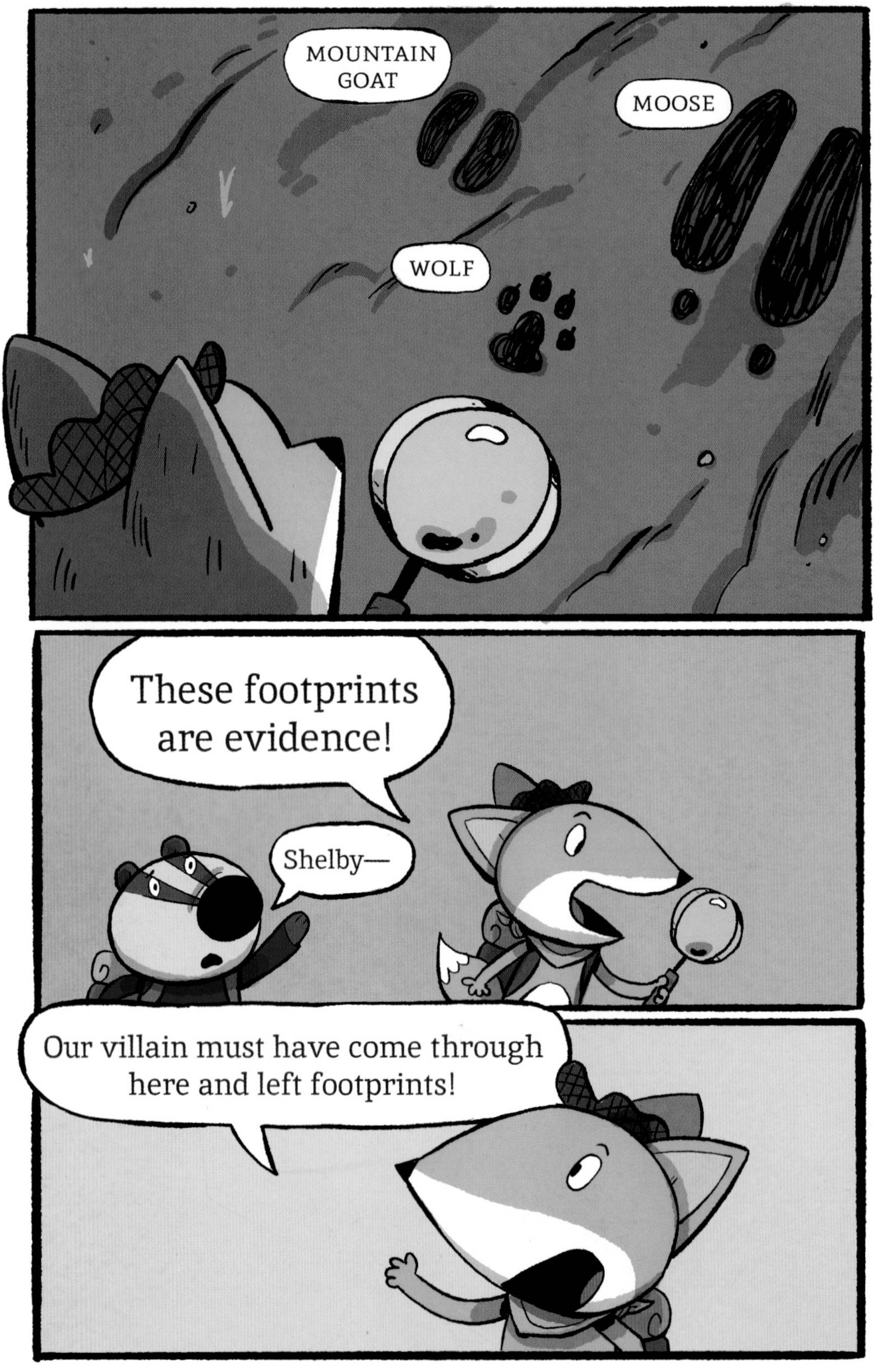
MOUNTAIN GOAT
MOOSE
WOLF
These footprints are evidence!
Shelby—
Our villain must have come through here and left footprints!

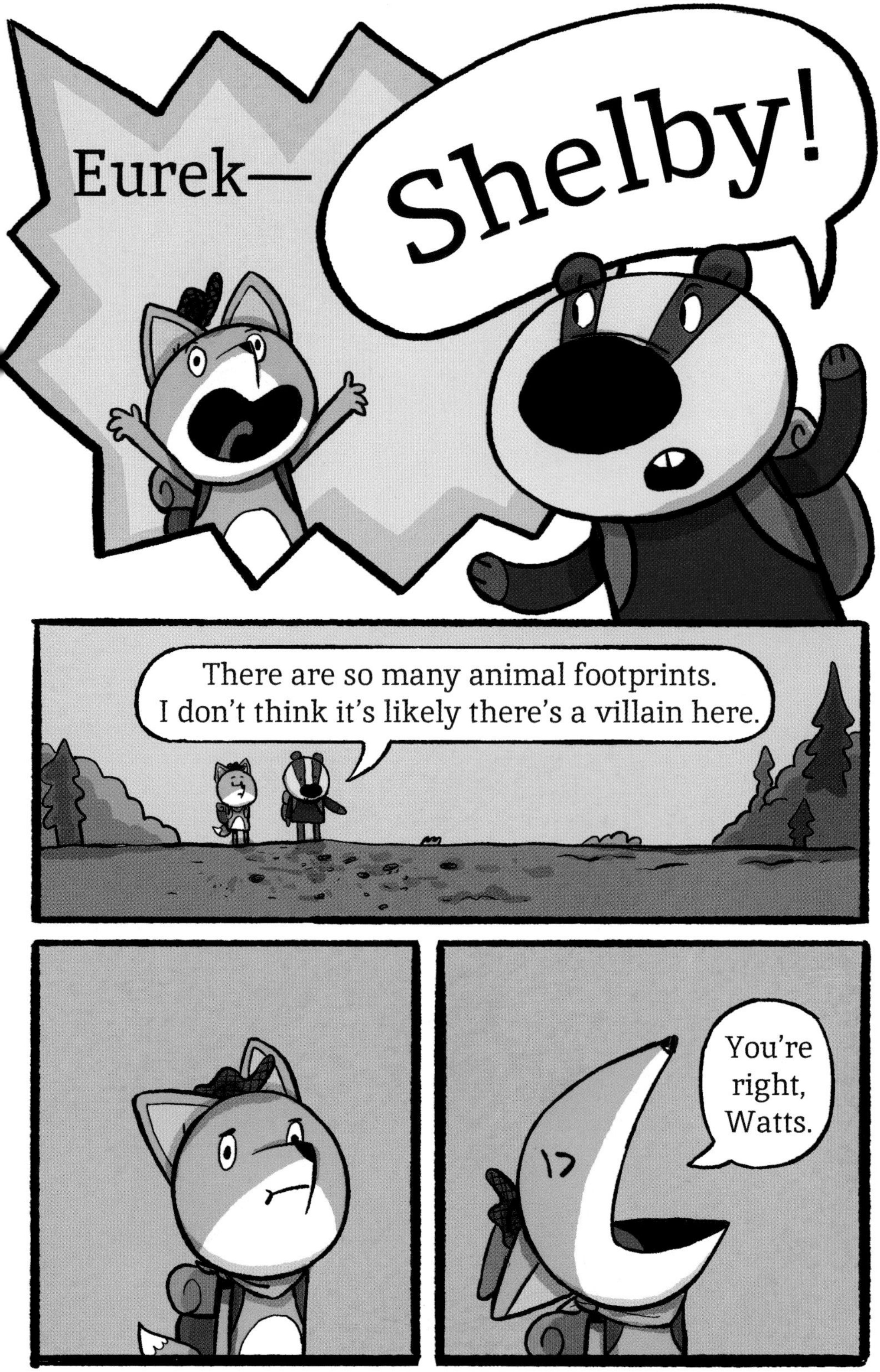
Eurek—
Shelby!
There are so many animal footprints. I don't think it's likely there's a villain here.
You're right, Watts.

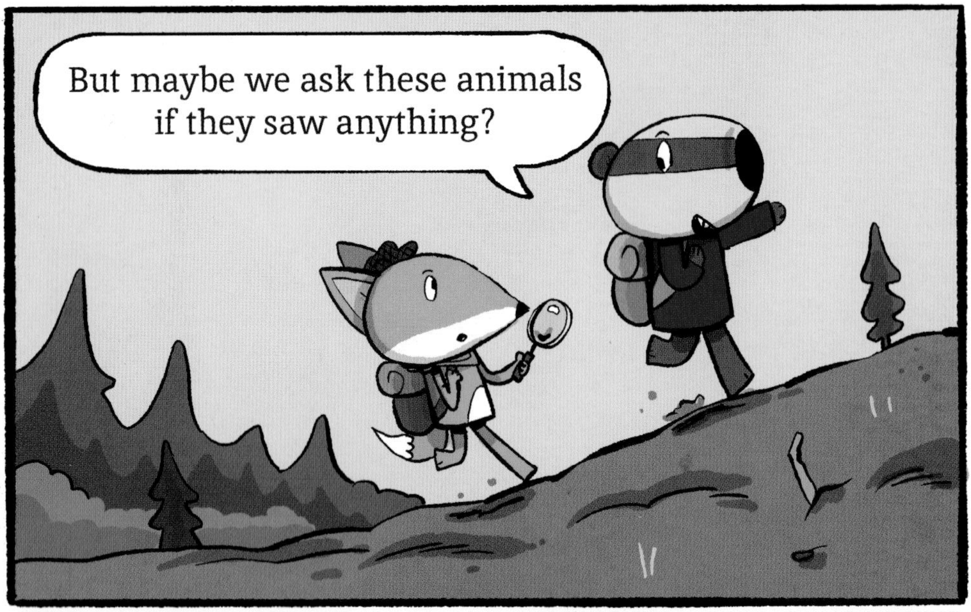
But maybe we ask these animals if they saw anything?

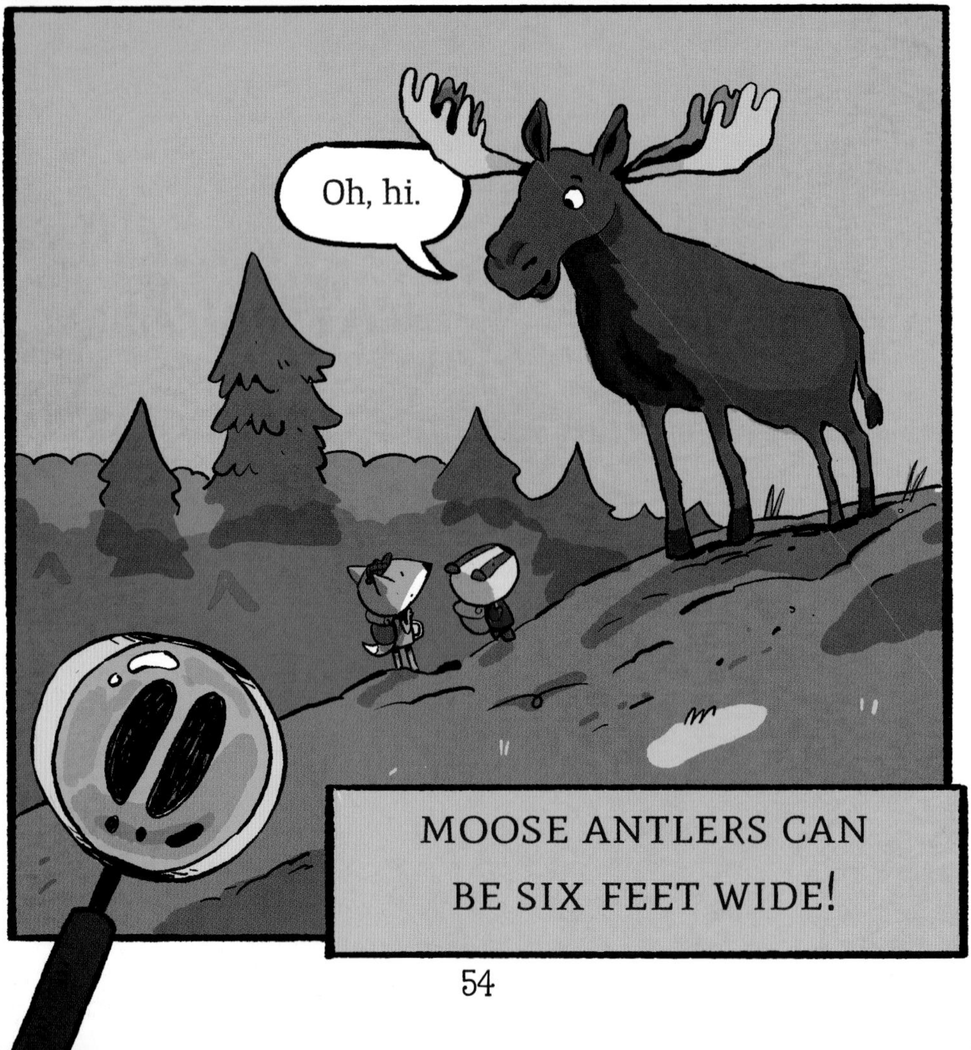
Oh, hi.
MOOSE ANTLERS CAN BE SIX FEET WIDE!

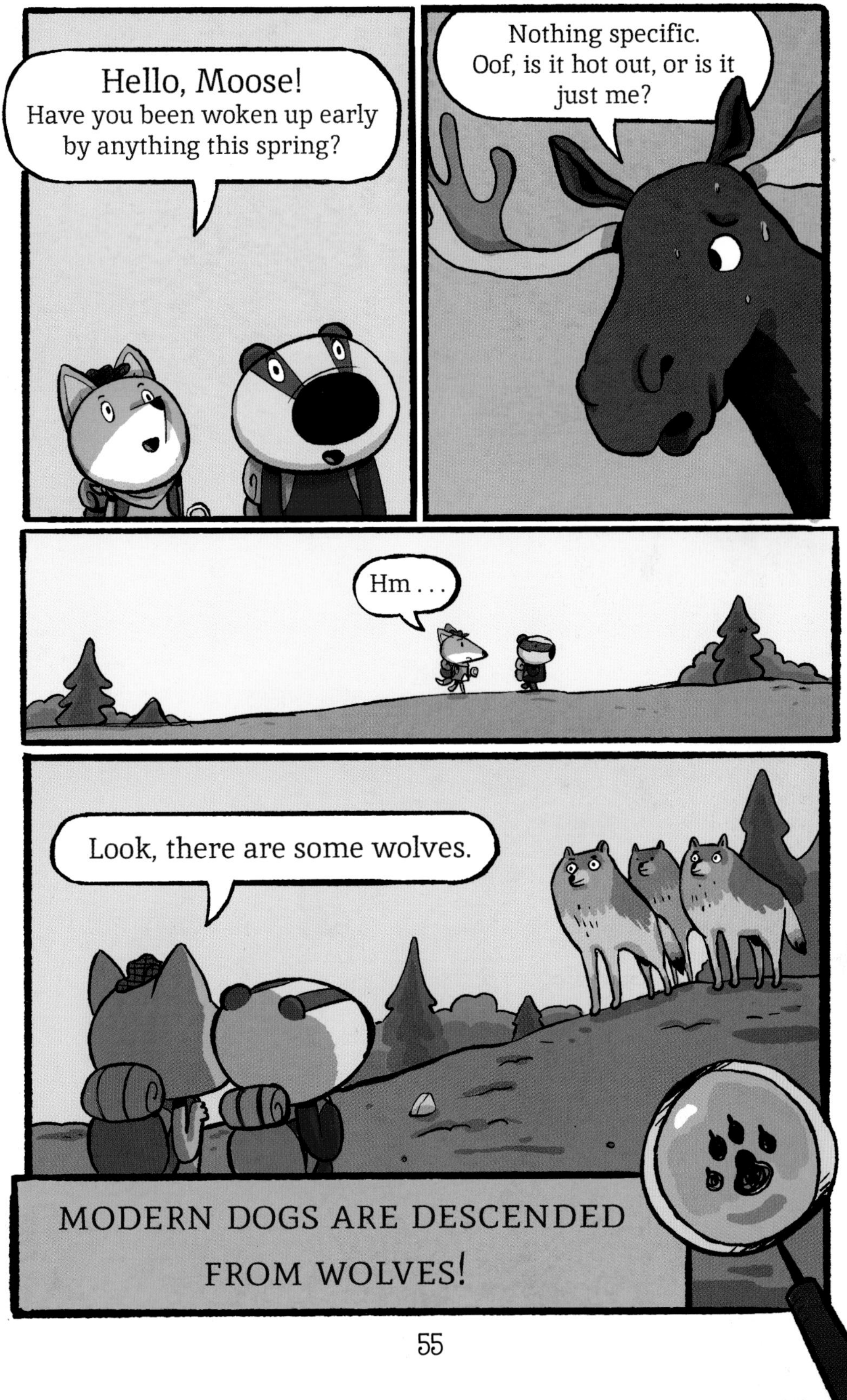
Hello, Moose!
Have you been woken up early by anything this spring?
Nothing specific.
Oof, is it hot out, or is it just me?
Hm . . .
Look, there are some wolves.
MODERN DOGS ARE DESCENDED FROM WOLVES!

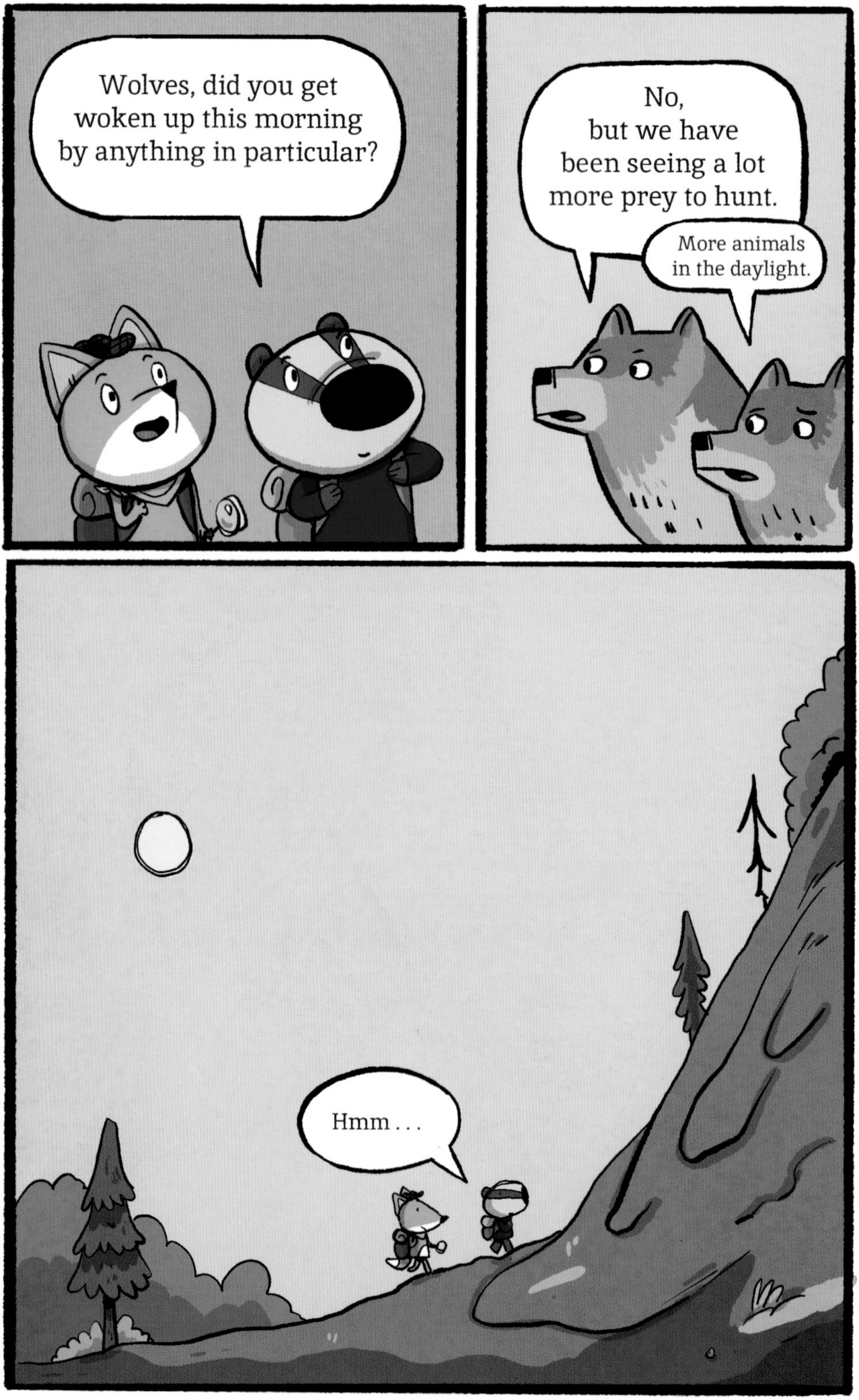
Wolves, did you get woken up this morning by anything in particular?
No, but we have been seeing a lot more prey to hunt.
More animals in the daylight.
Hmm . . .

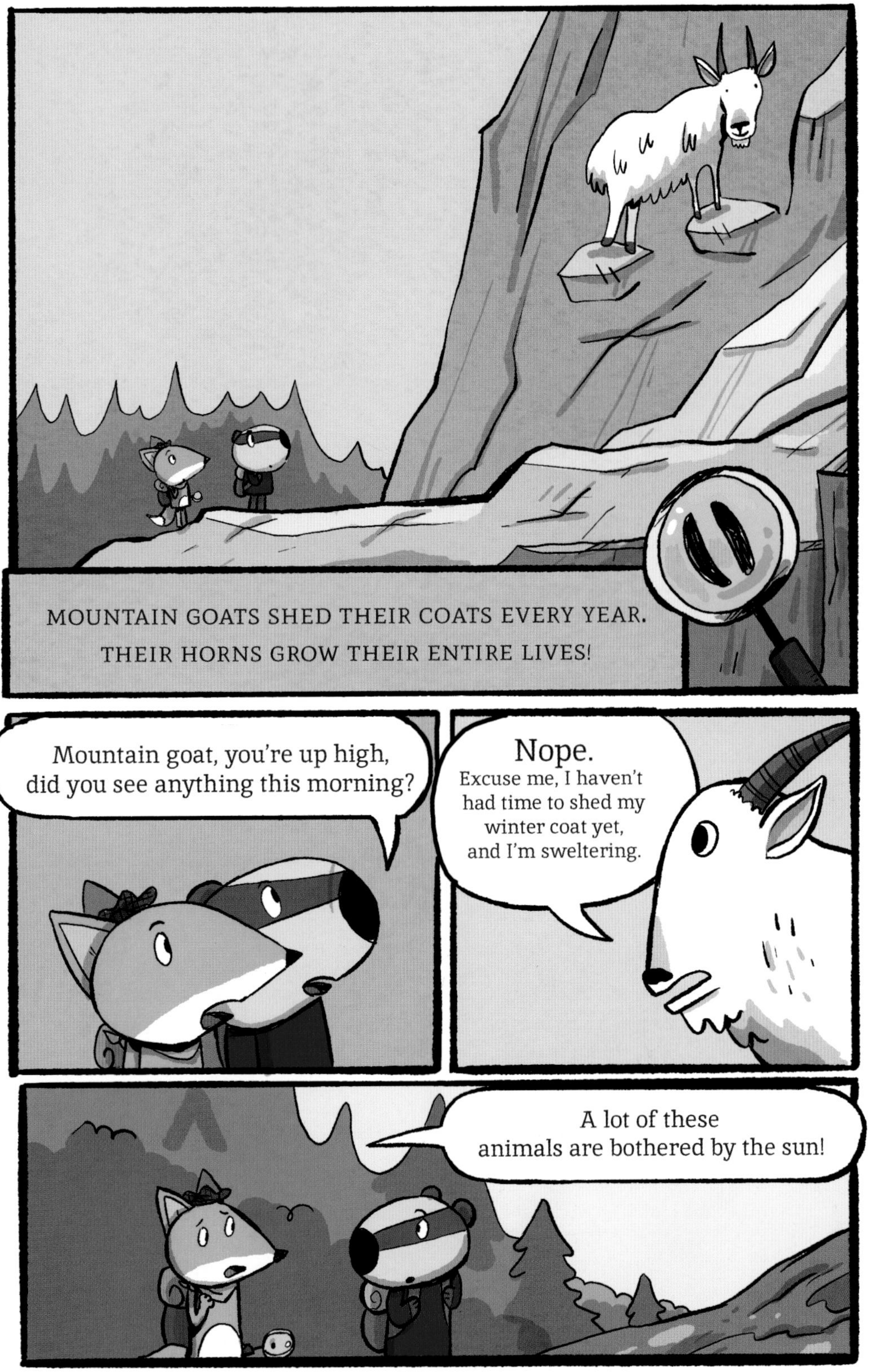
MOUNTAIN GOATS SHED THEIR COATS EVERY YEAR. THEIR HORNS GROW THEIR ENTIRE LIVES!
Mountain goat, you're up high, did you see anything this morning?
Nope. Excuse me, I haven't had time to shed my winter coat yet, and I'm sweltering.
A lot of these animals are bothered by the sun!

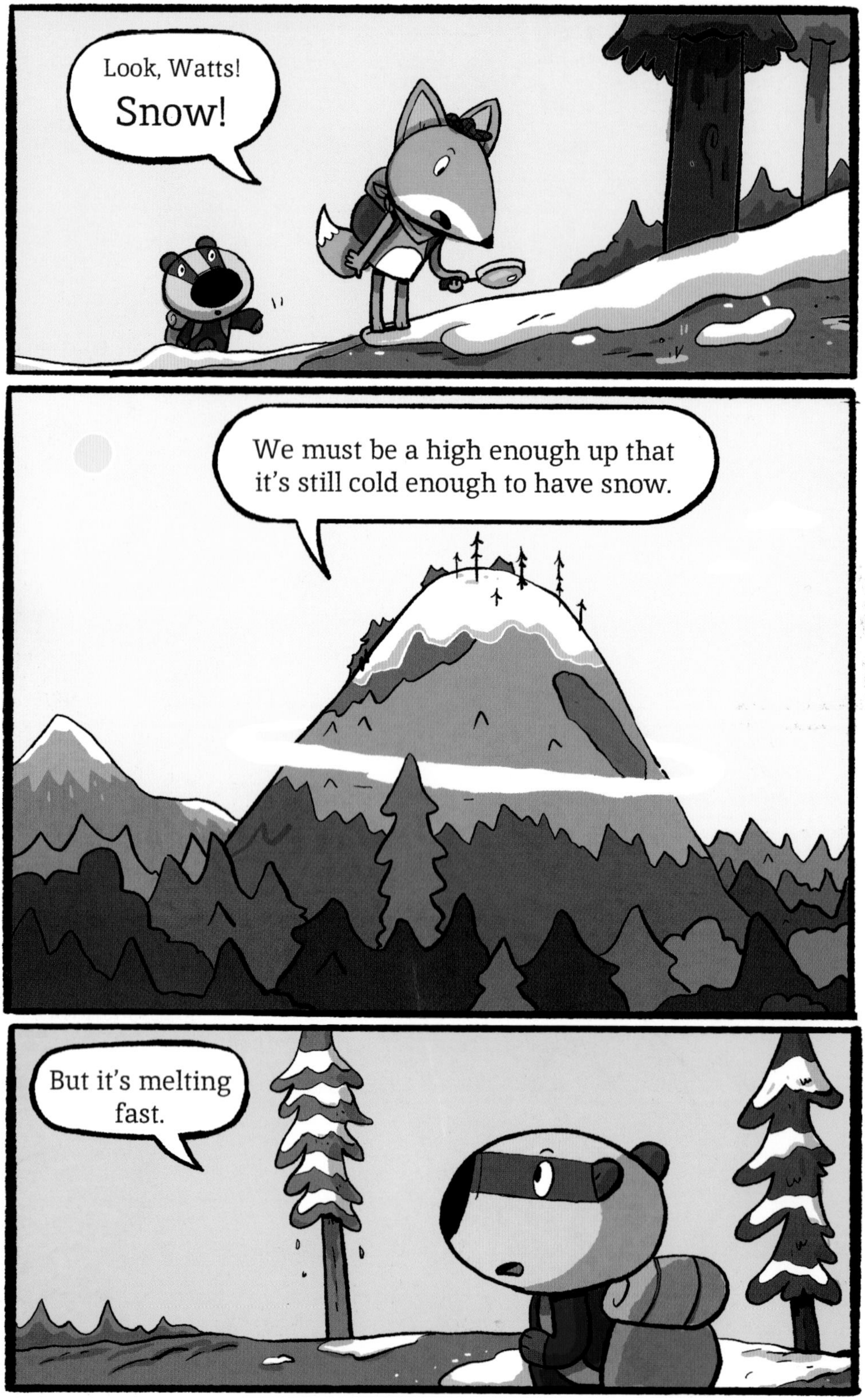
Look, Watts! Snow!
We must be a high enough up that it's still cold enough to have snow.
But it's melting fast.

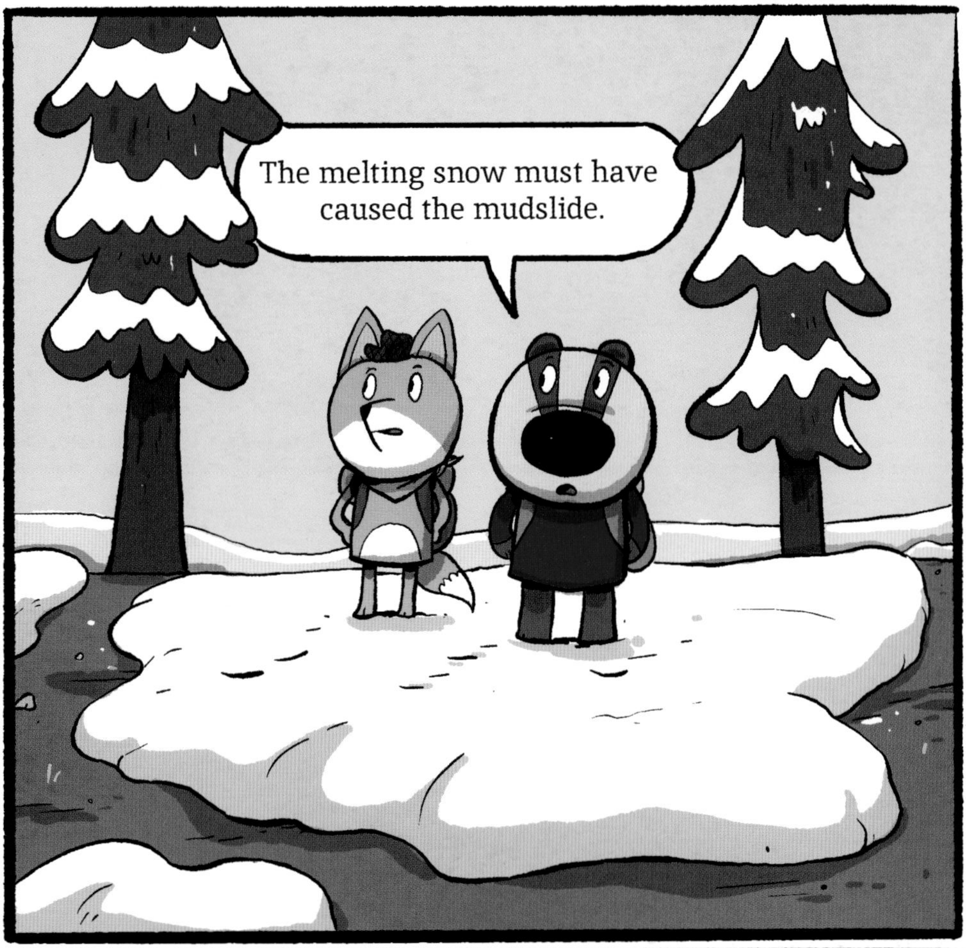
The melting snow must have caused the mudslide.

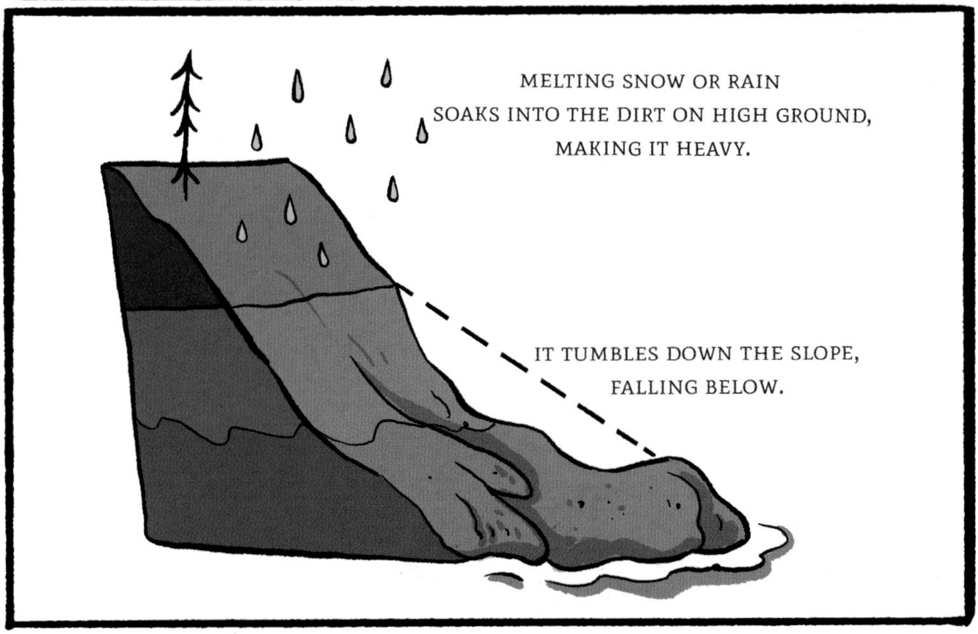
MELTING SNOW OR RAIN SOAKS INTO THE DIRT ON HIGH GROUND, MAKING IT HEAVY.
IT TUMBLES DOWN THE SLOPE, FALLING BELOW.

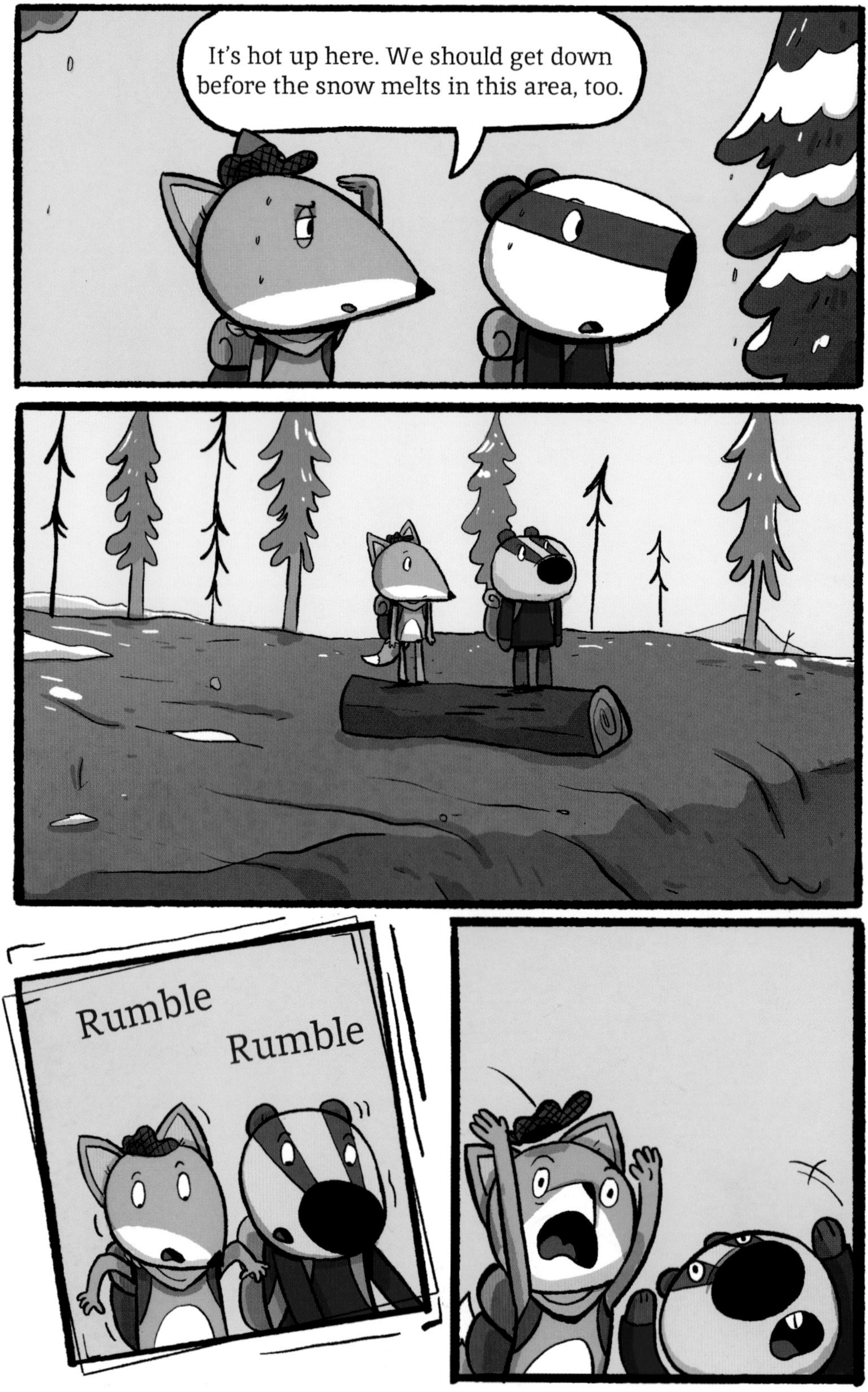
It's hot up here. We should get down before the snow melts in this area, too.
Rumble
Rumble

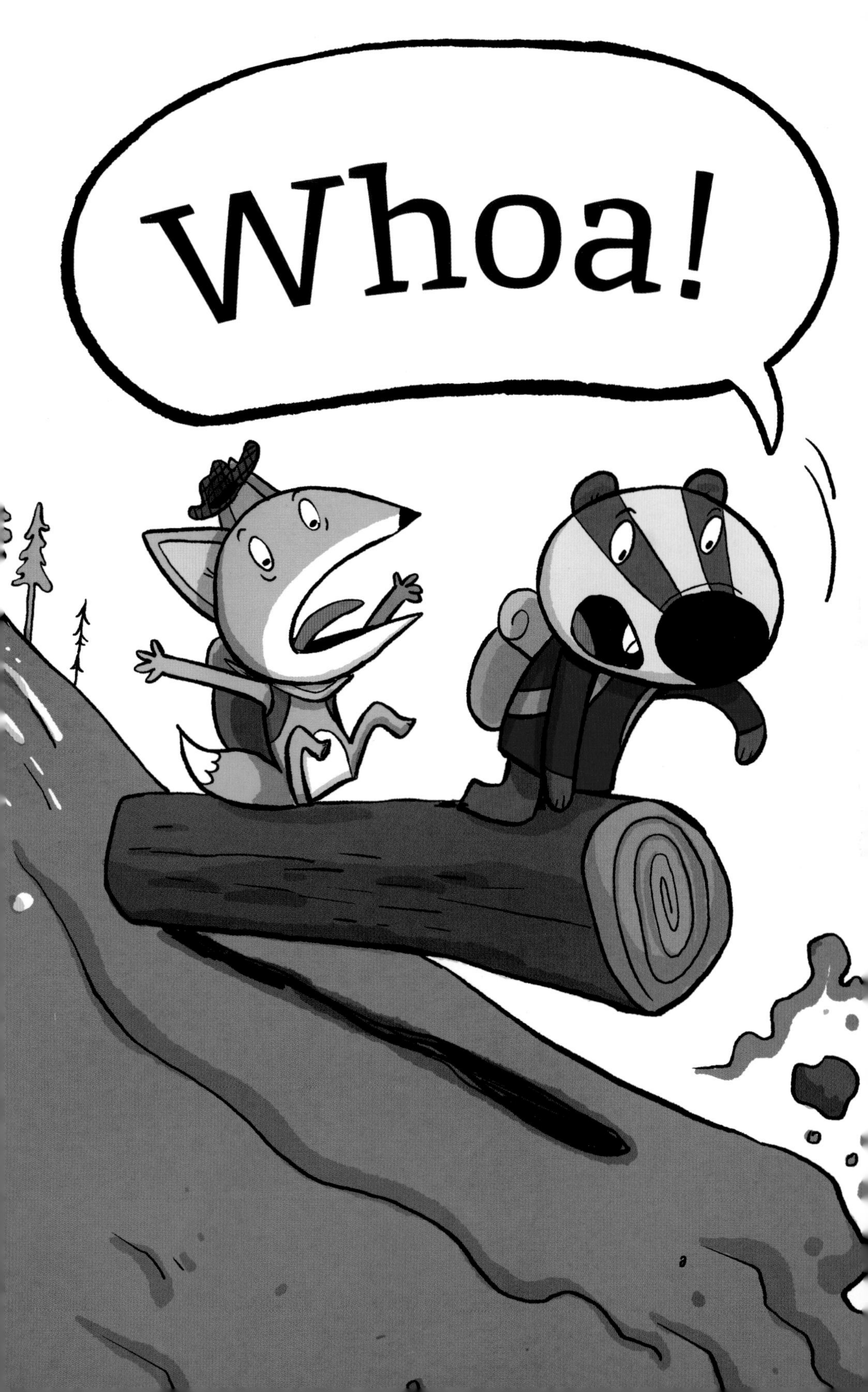
Whoa!

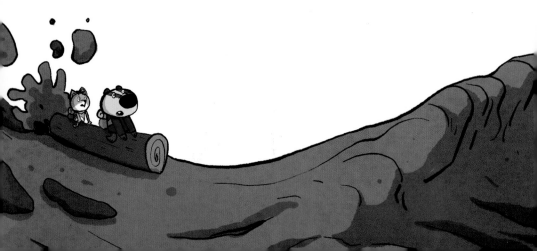

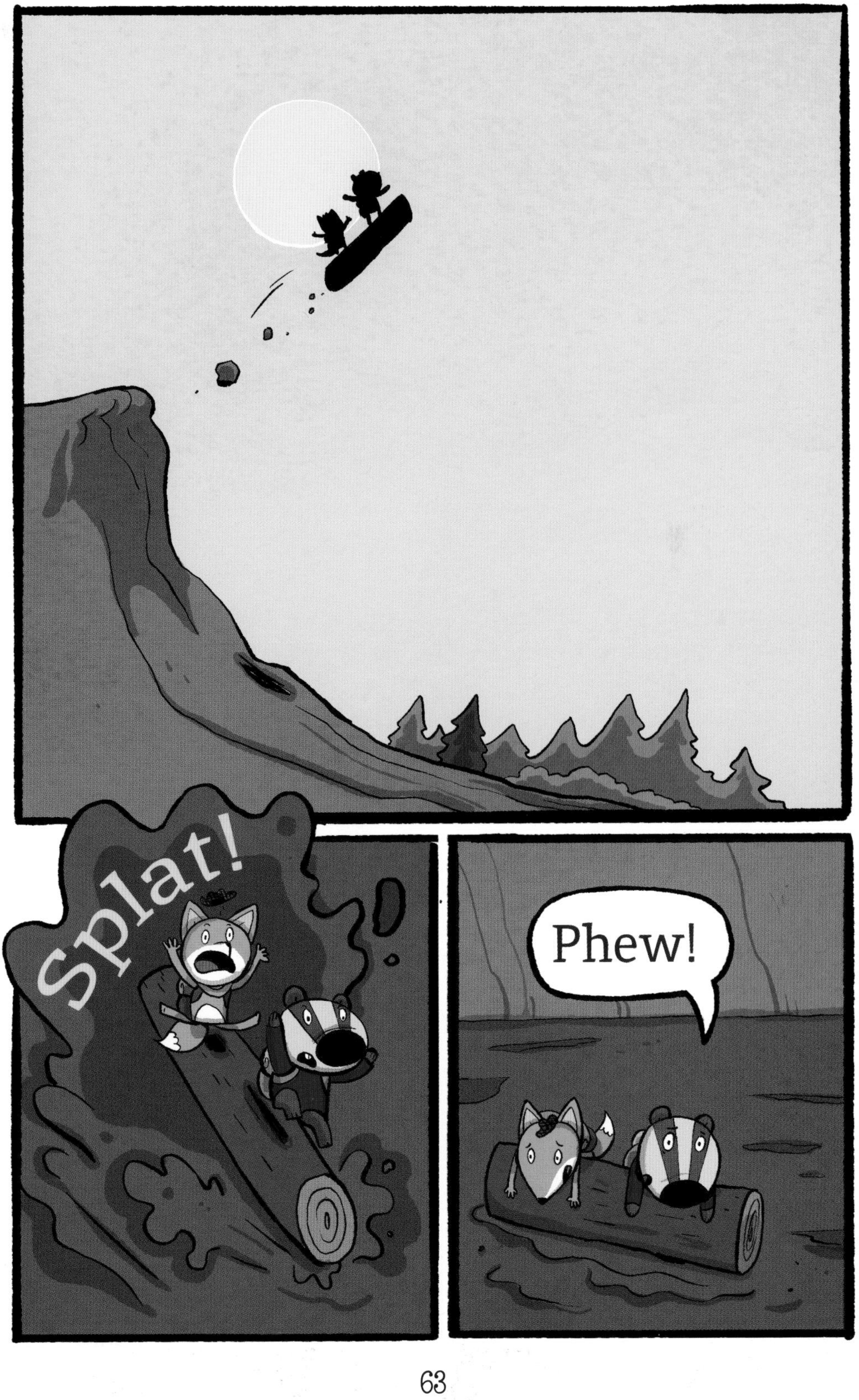
Splat!
Phew!

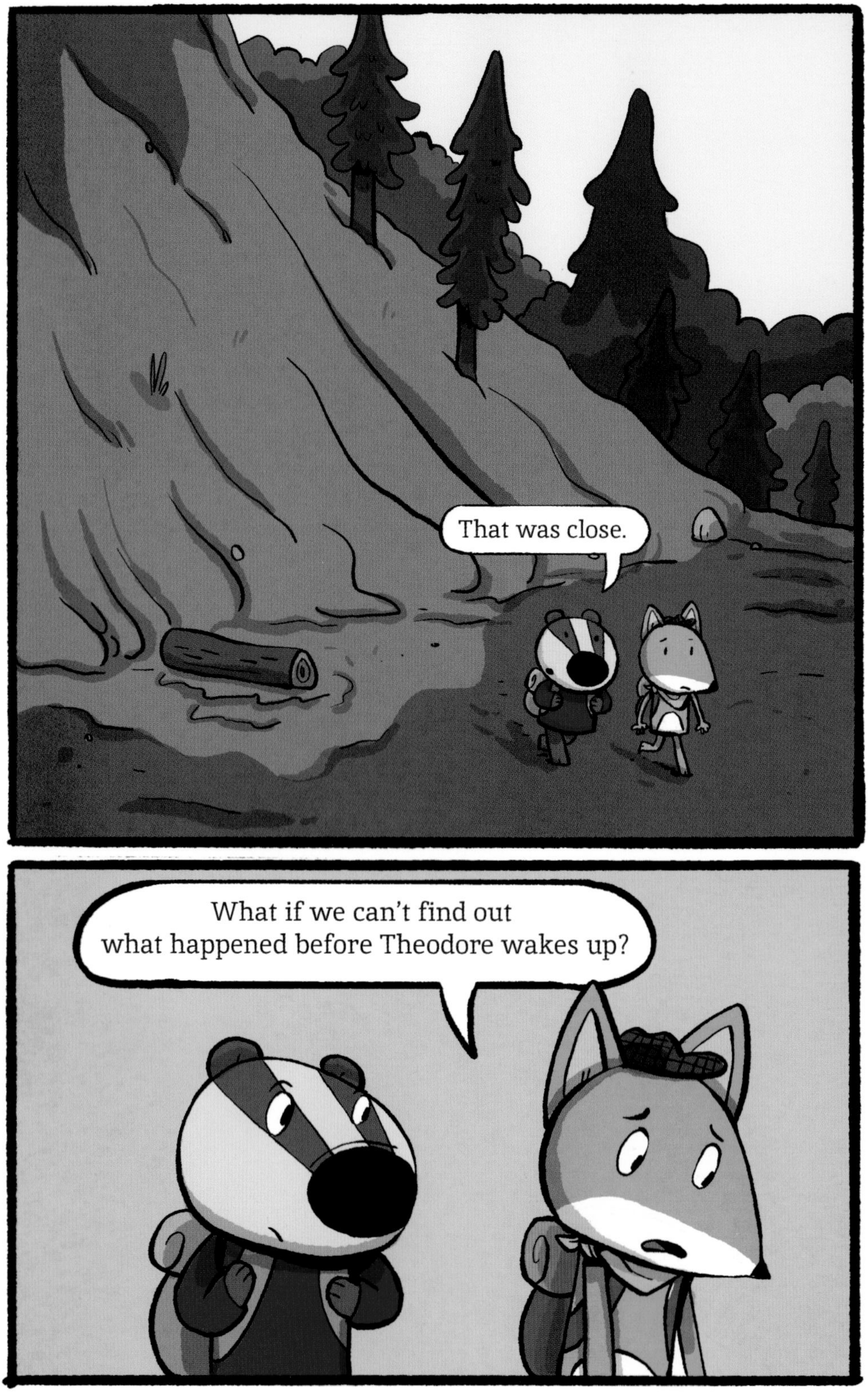
That was close.
What if we can't find out what happened before Theodore wakes up?

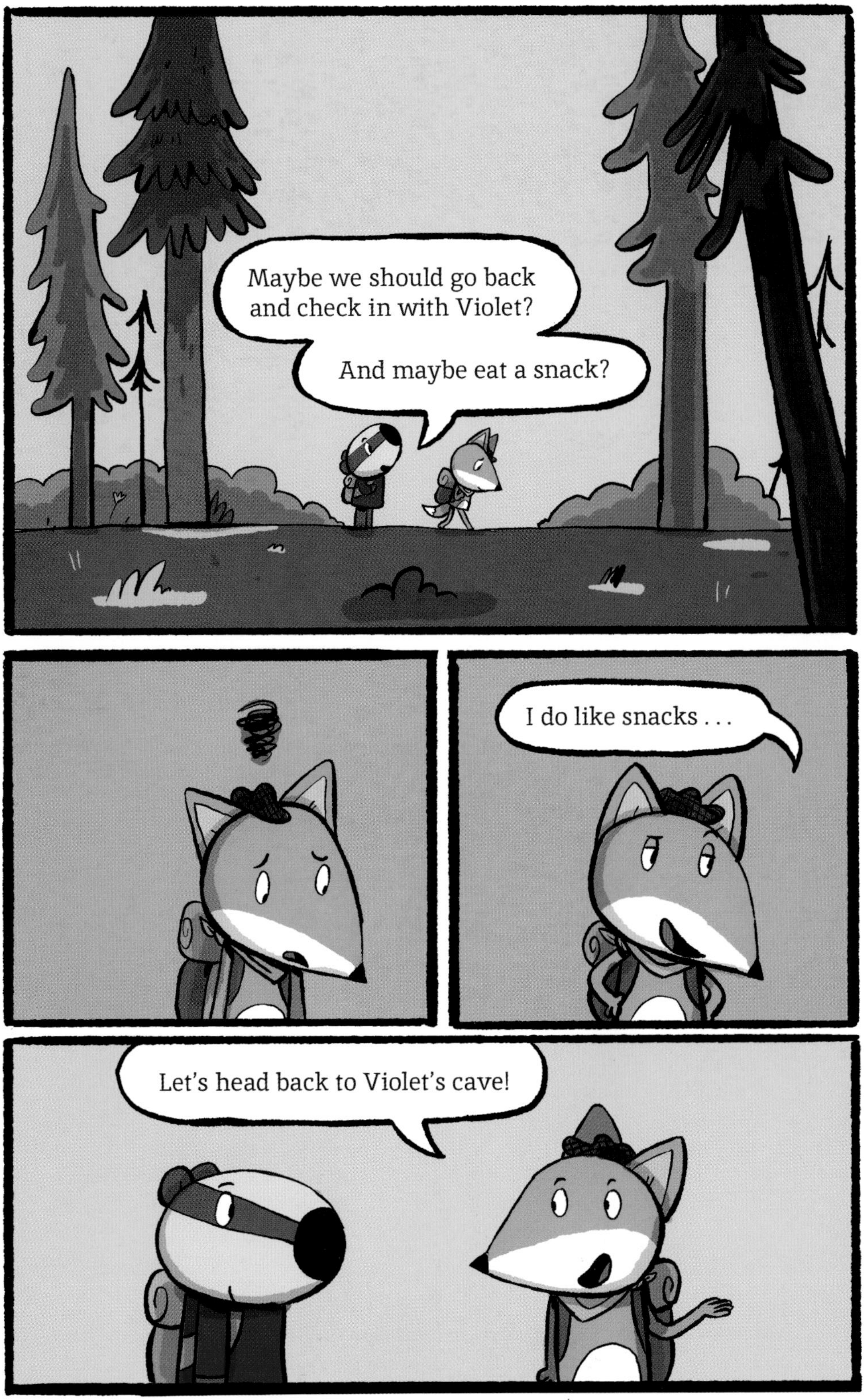
Maybe we should go back and check in with Violet?
And maybe eat a snack?
I do like snacks . . .
Let's head back to Violet's cave!

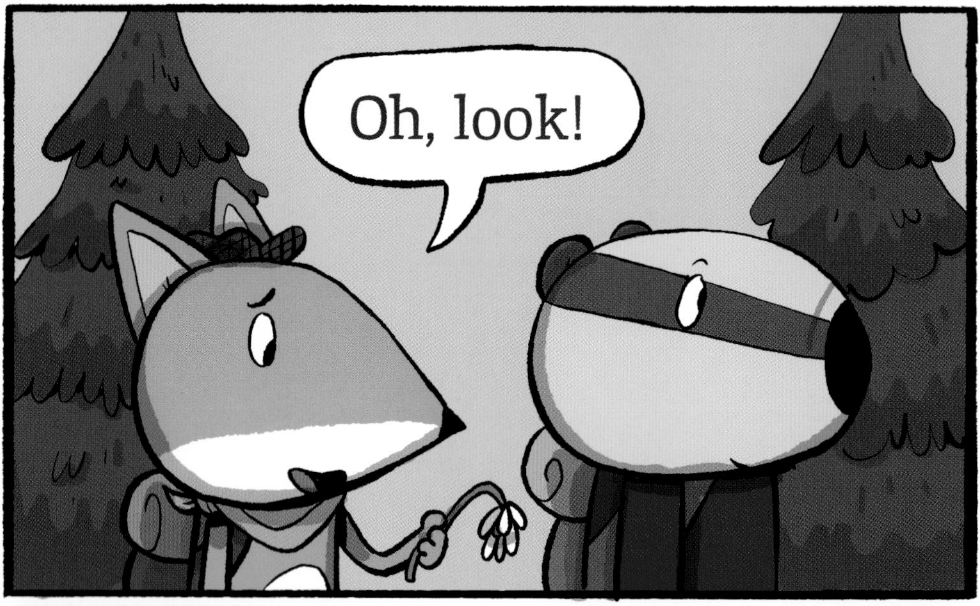
Oh, look!

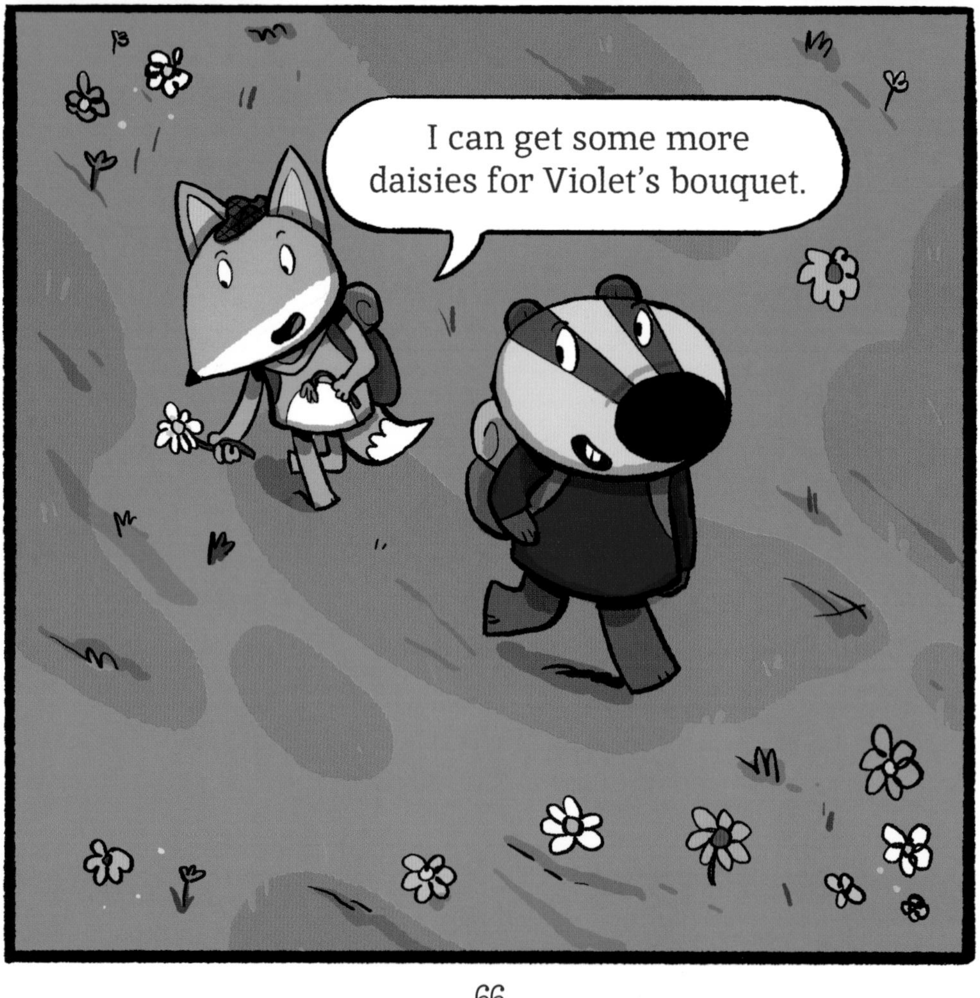
I can get some more daisies for Violet's bouquet.

CHAPTER 6

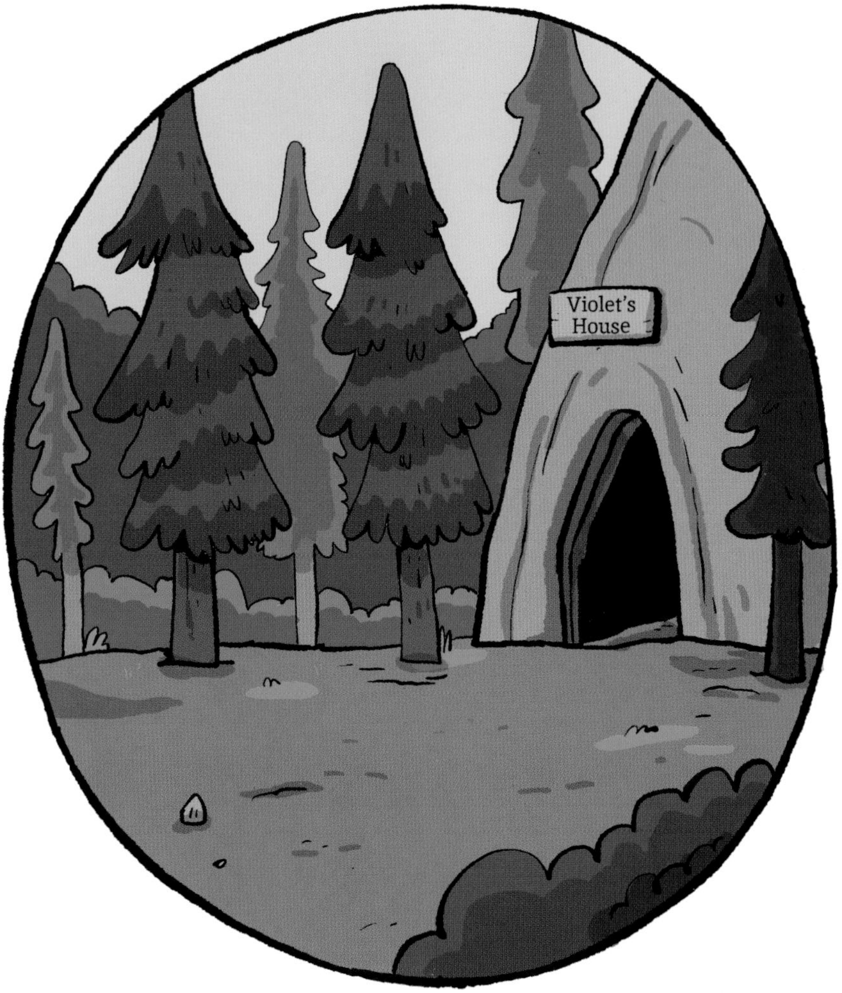
Violet's
House

Back at Violet's Cave . . .

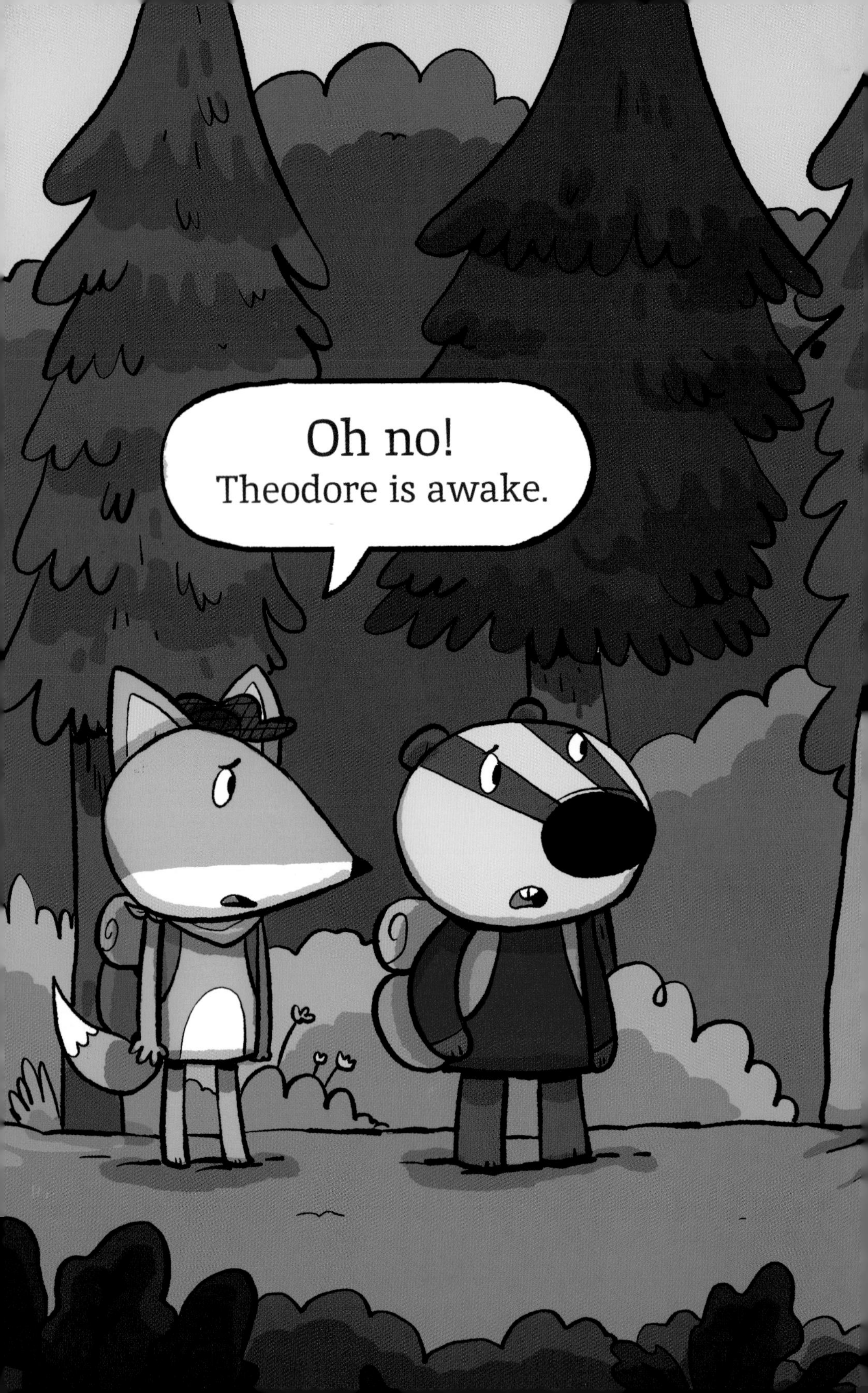
Oh no!
Theodore is awake.

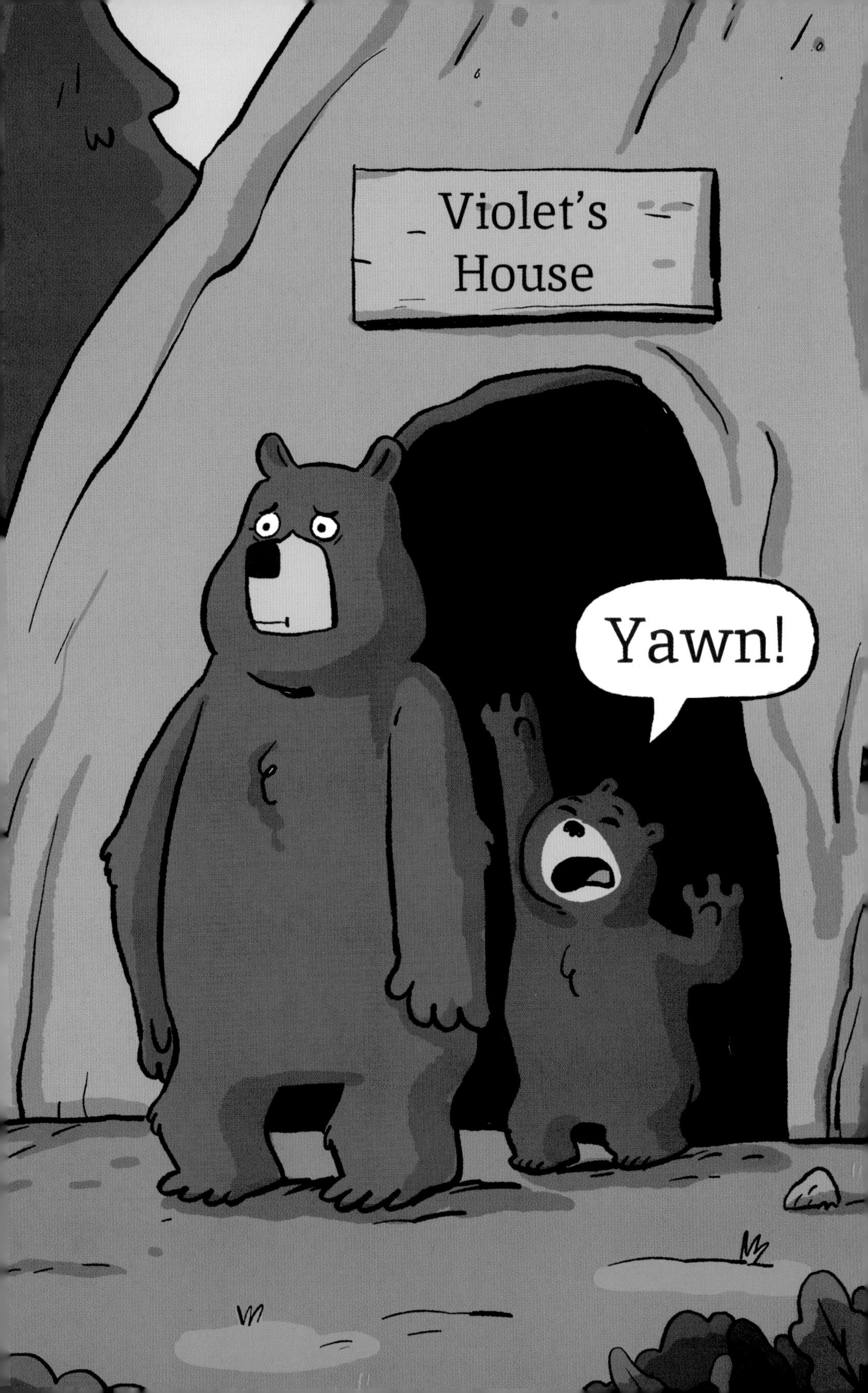
Violet's House
Yawn!

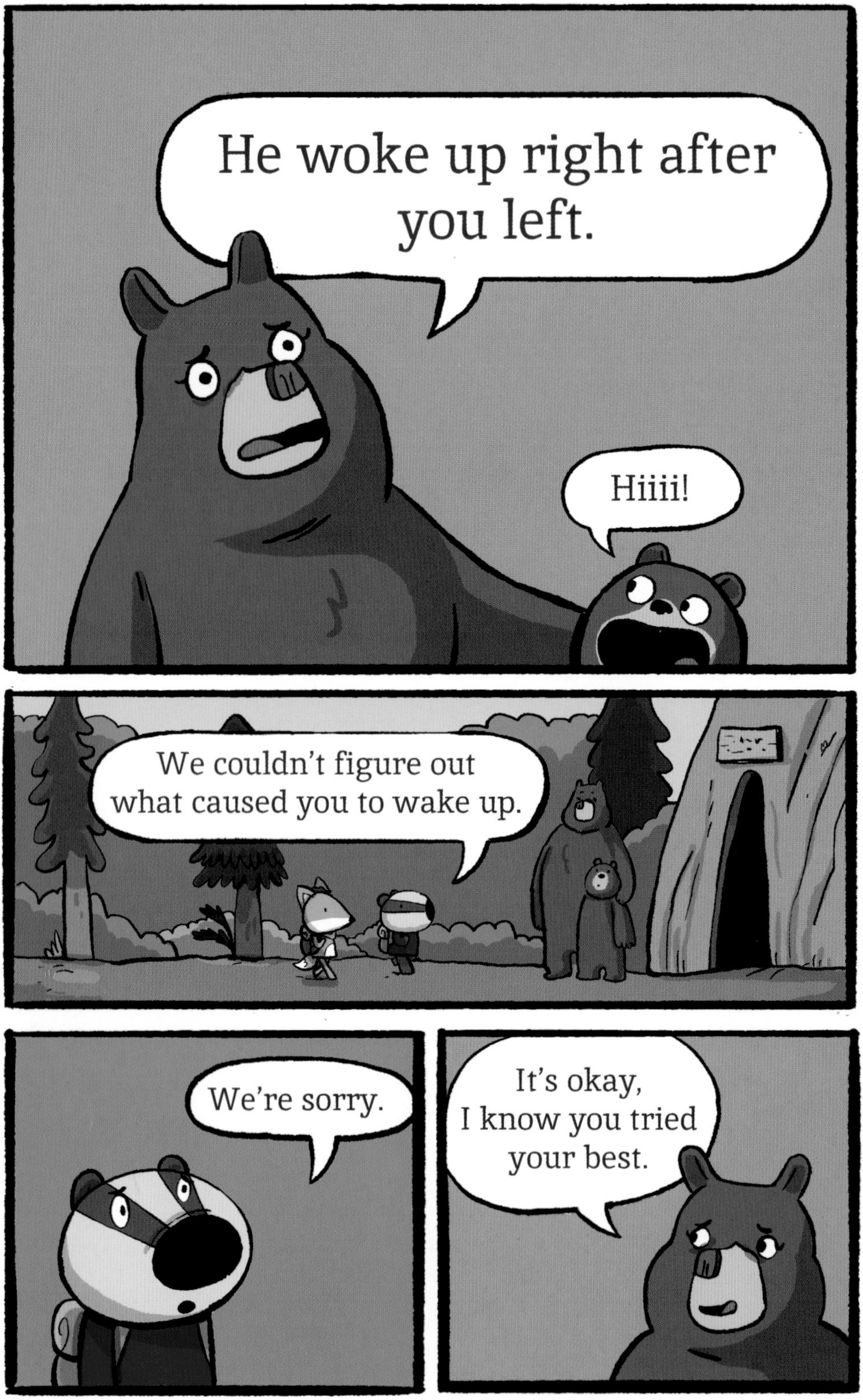
He woke up right after you left.
Hiiii!
We couldn't figure out what caused you to wake up.
We're sorry.
It's okay, I know you tried your best.

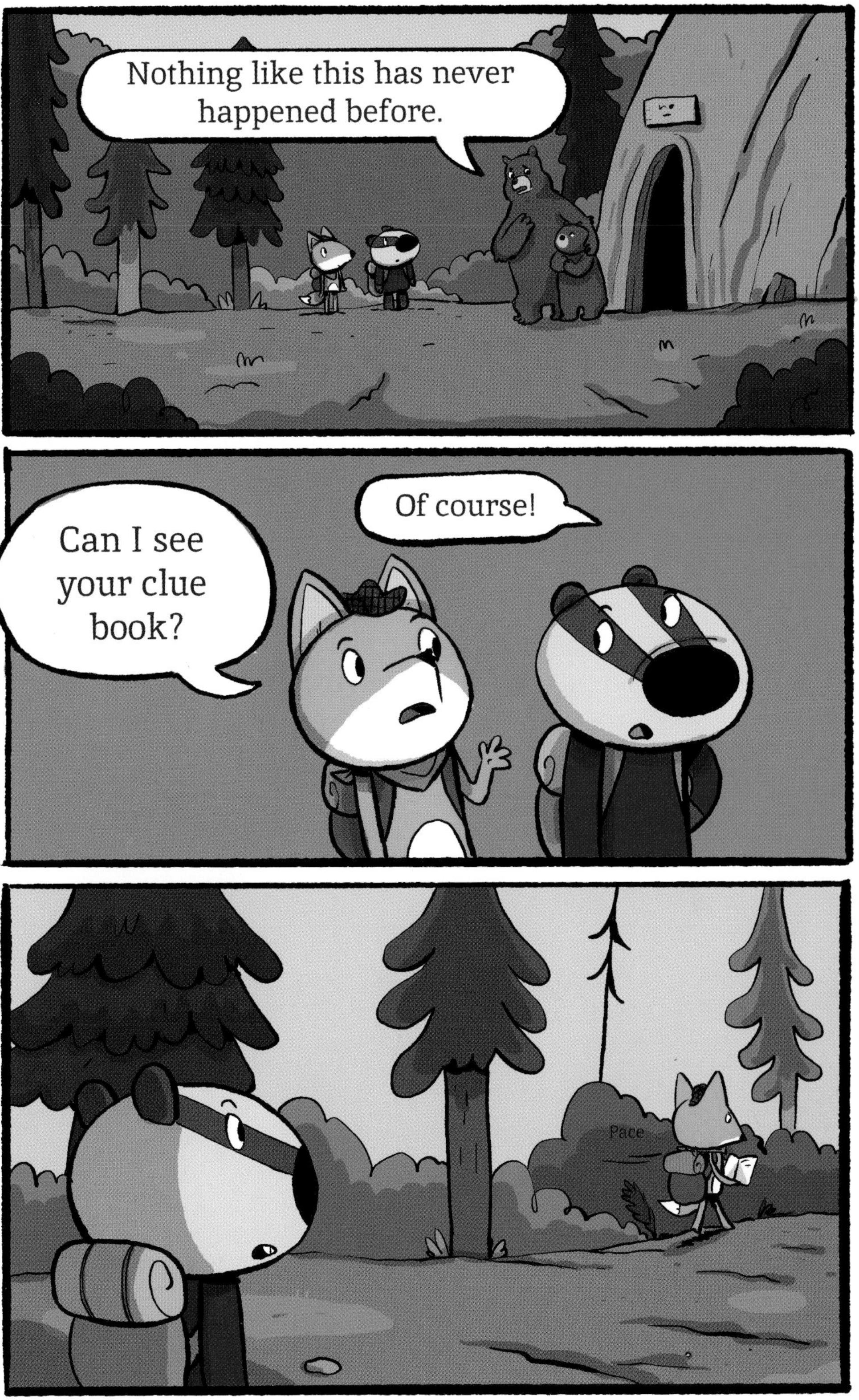
Nothing like this has never happened before.
Can I see your clue book?
Of course!
Pace

CLUES

VIOLET'S CAVE

VIOLET WOKEN
FROM HIBERNATION EARLY

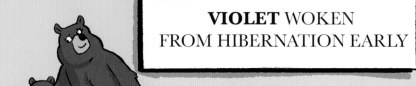

THEODORE
WOKEN UP TOO

OTHER ANIMALS
NOTICED CHANGES

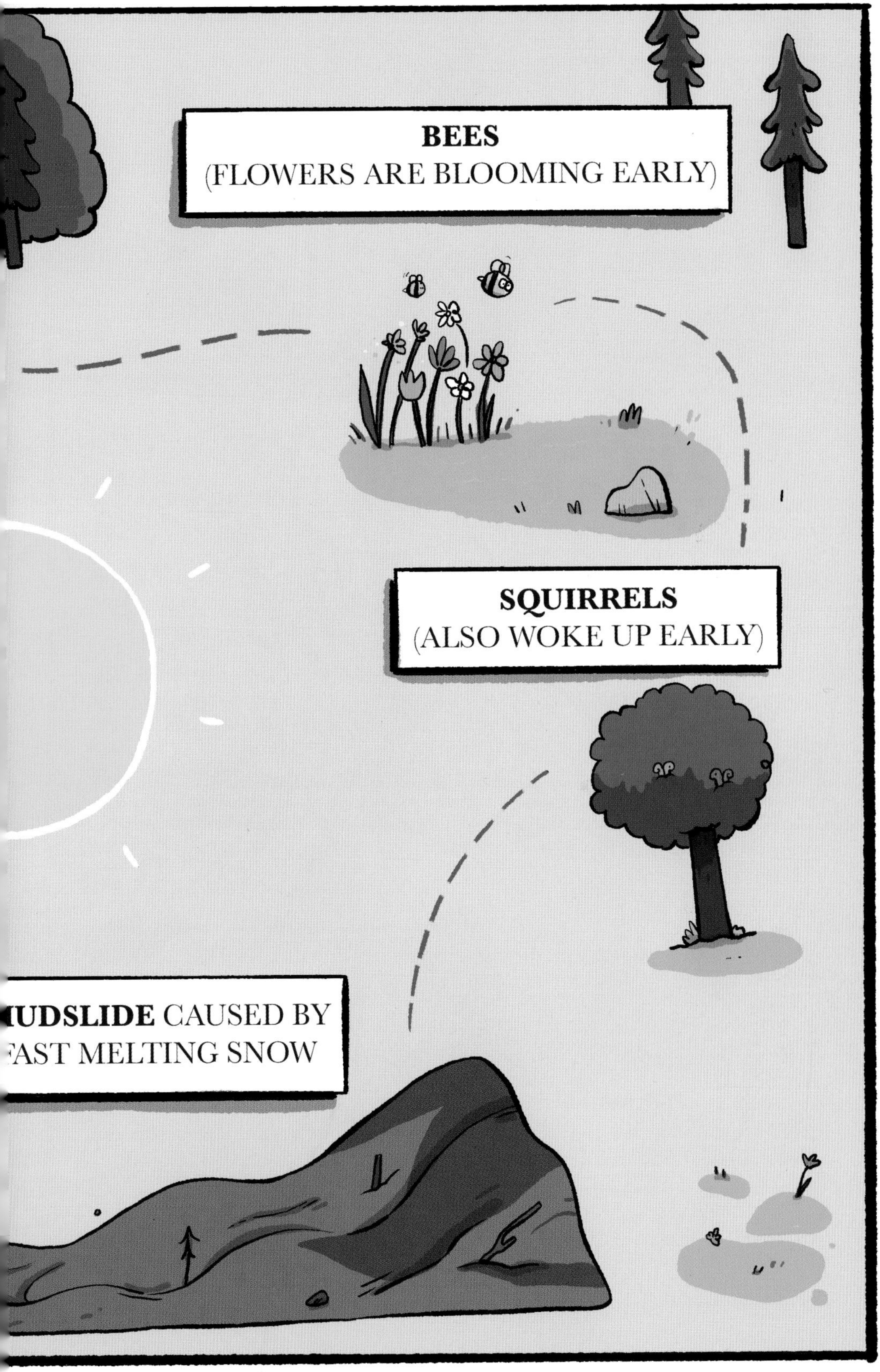
BEES
(FLOWERS ARE BLOOMING EARLY)
SQUIRRELS
(ALSO WOKE UP EARLY)
UDSLIDE CAUSED BY
AST MELTING SNOW

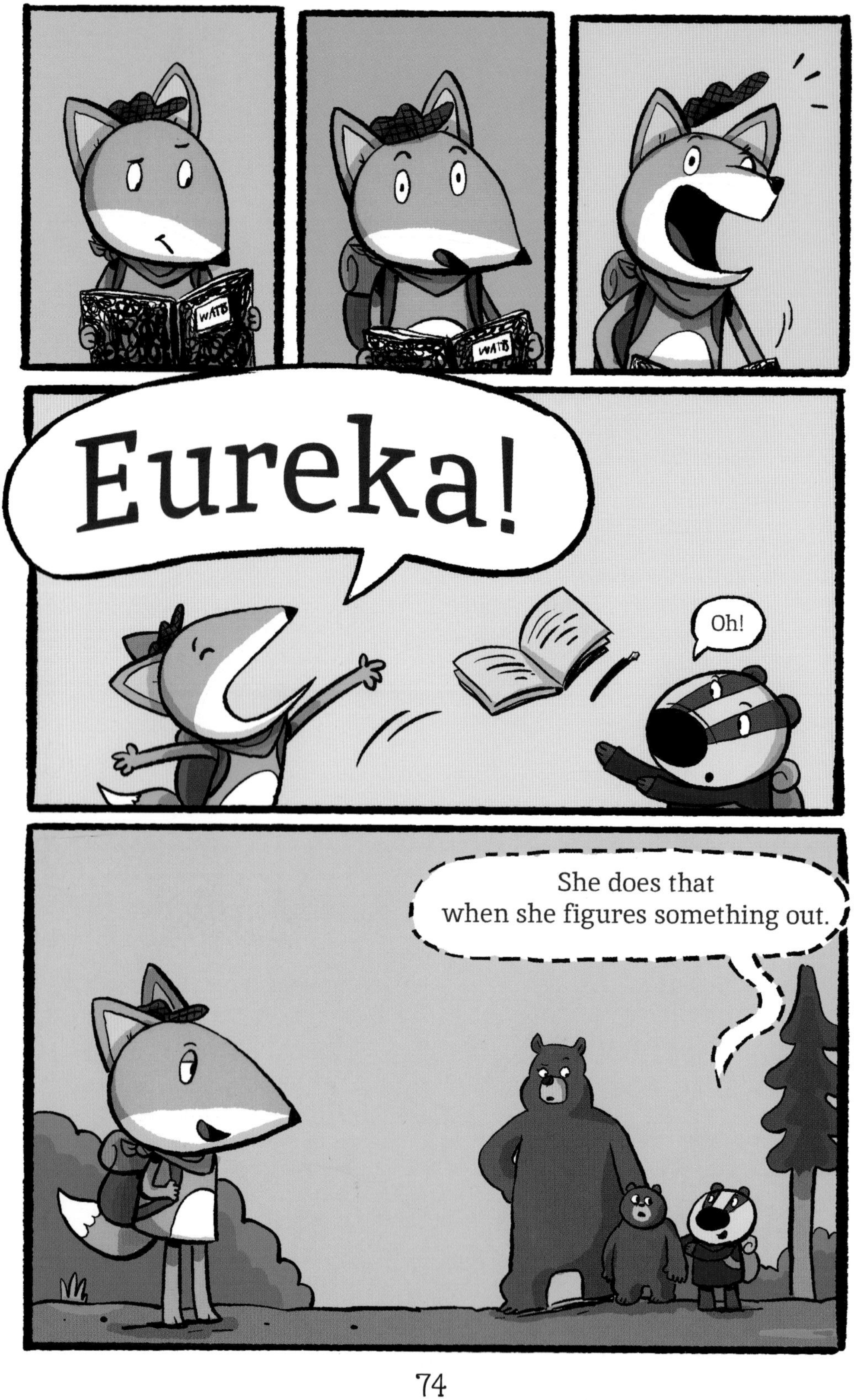

Eureka!
Oh!
She does that when she figures something out.

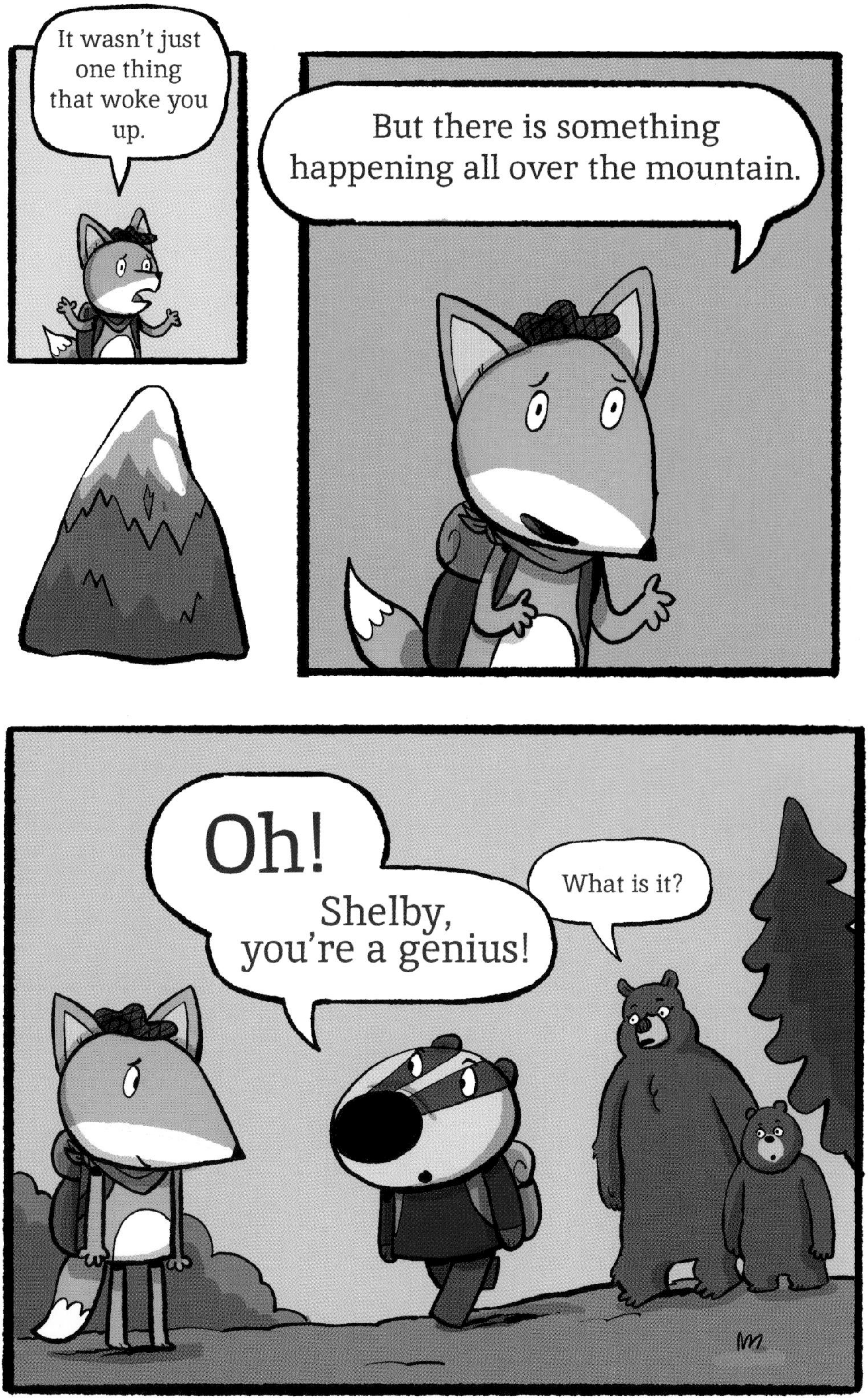
It wasn't just one thing that woke you up.
But there is something happening all over the mountain.
Oh!
Shelby, you're a genius!
What is it?

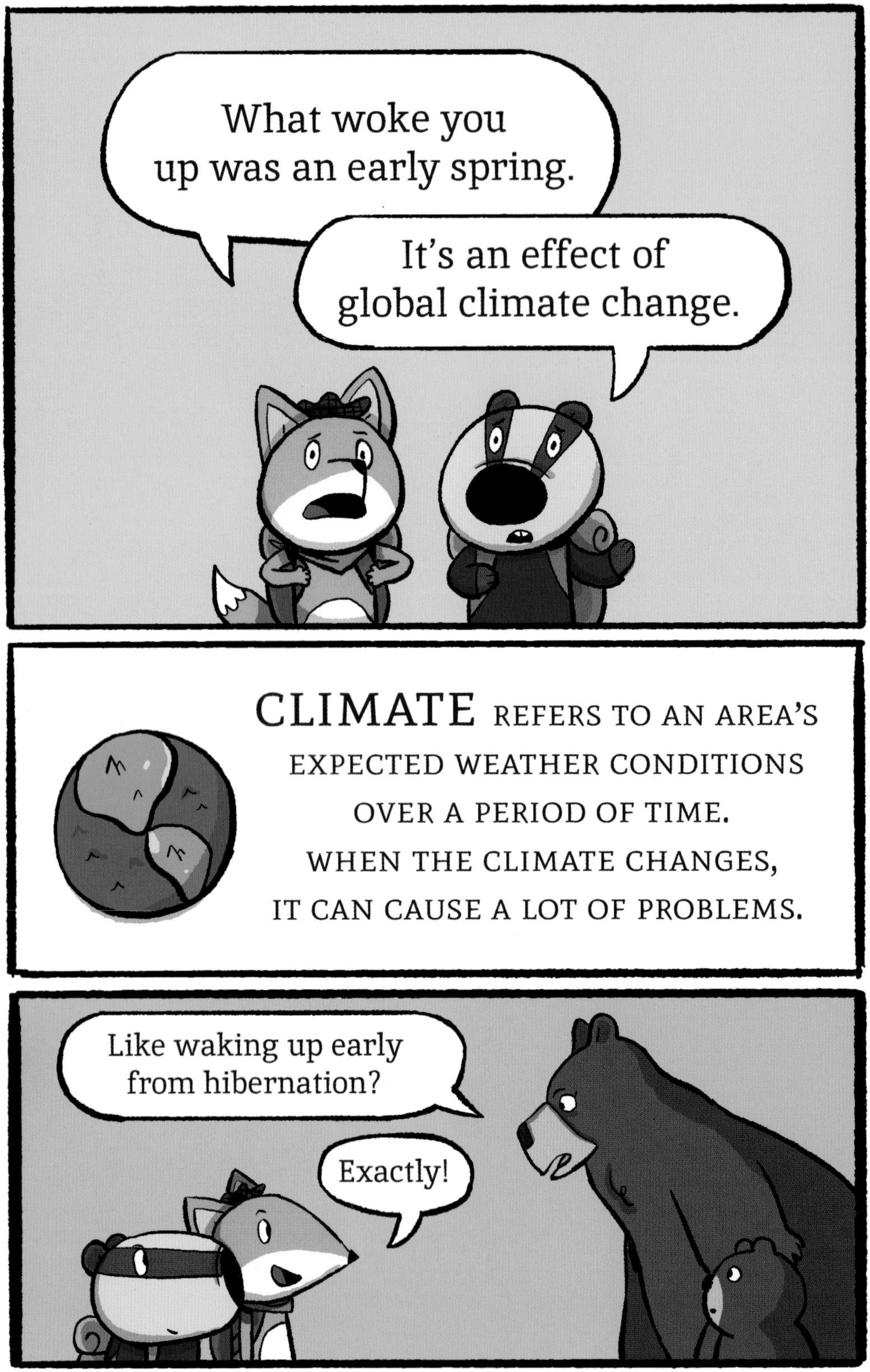
What woke you up was an early spring.
It's an effect of global climate change.
CLIMATE REFERS TO AN AREA'S EXPECTED WEATHER CONDITIONS OVER A PERIOD OF TIME. WHEN THE CLIMATE CHANGES, IT CAN CAUSE A LOT OF PROBLEMS.
Like waking up early from hibernation?
Exactly!

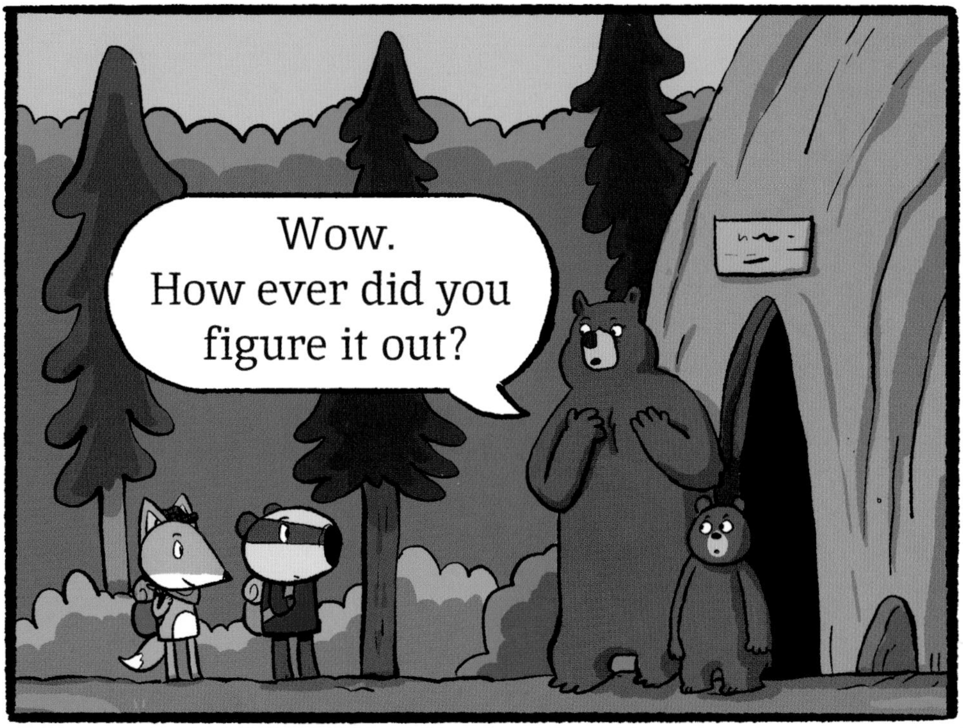
Wow.
How ever did you
figure it out?

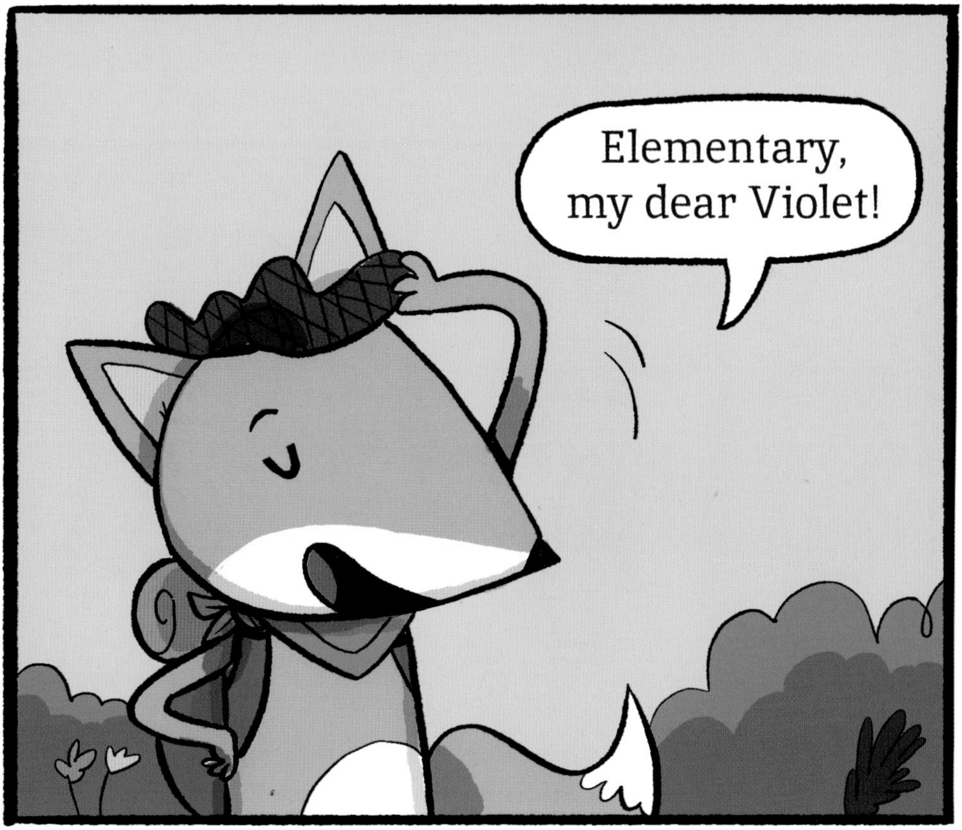
Elementary,
my dear Violet!

The Case of the Not-So-Sleepy Bears

I first noticed something was strange in Valley Glen, when it was very hot, even for a spring day.

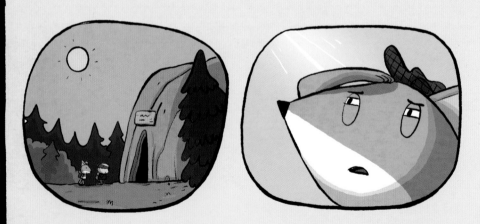

When we got to your cave, it was also bright and hot.

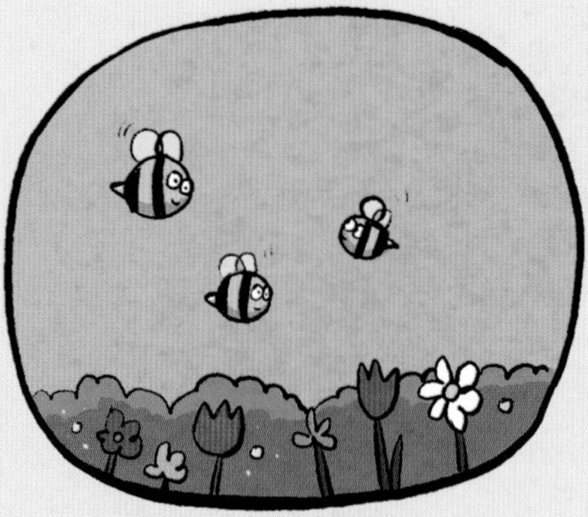

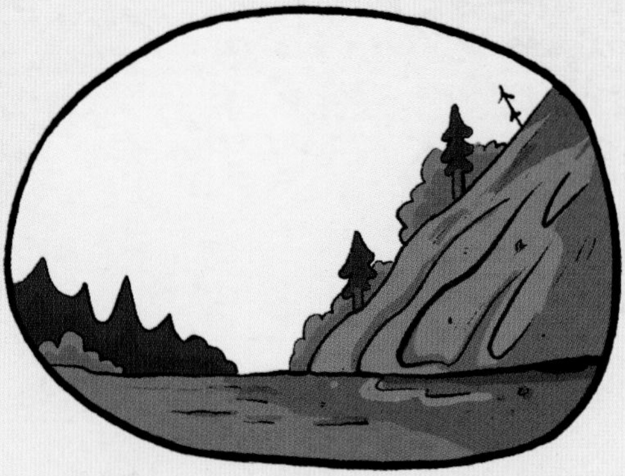

We followed clues around the mountain, and noticed that there were a lot of unexpected changes—like the flowers blooming early.

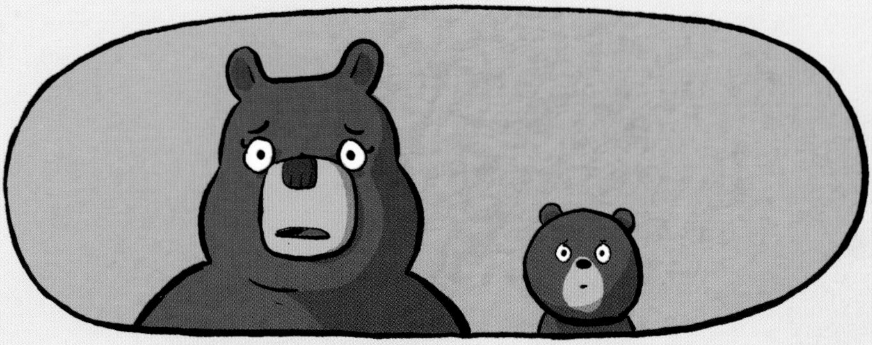

Finally, you mentioned that nothing like this had happened before, which is when I realized that the climate of the mountain had changed.

Solved!

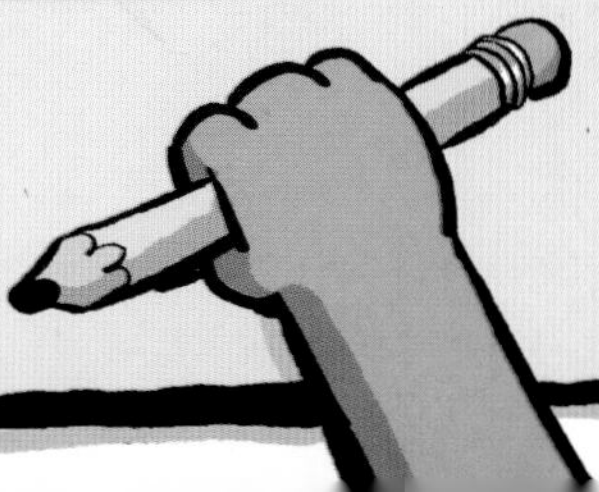

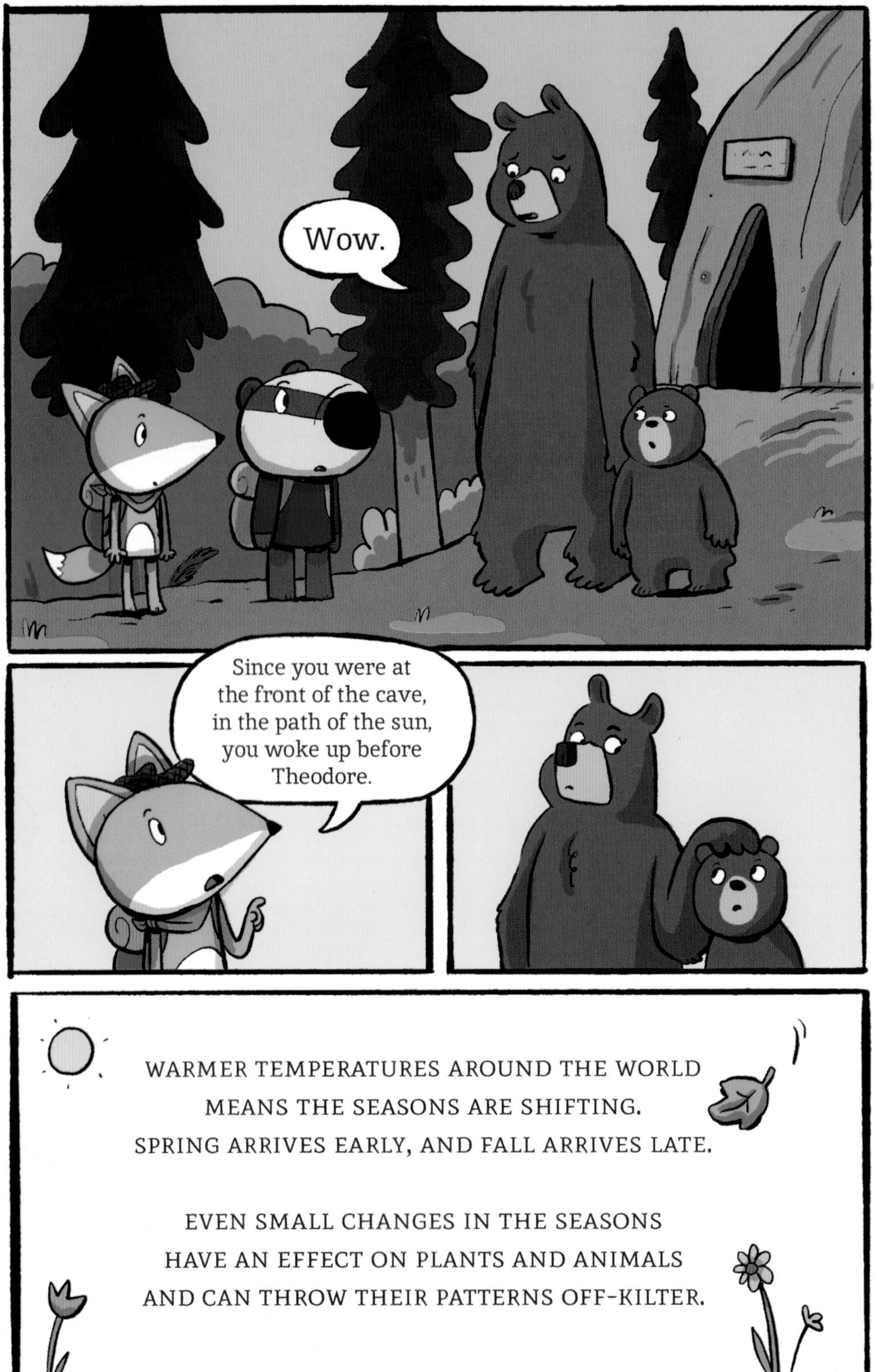
Wow.
Since you were at the front of the cave, in the path of the sun, you woke up before Theodore.
WARMER TEMPERATURES AROUND THE WORLD MEANS THE SEASONS ARE SHIFTING. SPRING ARRIVES EARLY, AND FALL ARRIVES LATE.
EVEN SMALL CHANGES IN THE SEASONS HAVE AN EFFECT ON PLANTS AND ANIMALS AND CAN THROW THEIR PATTERNS OFF-KILTER.

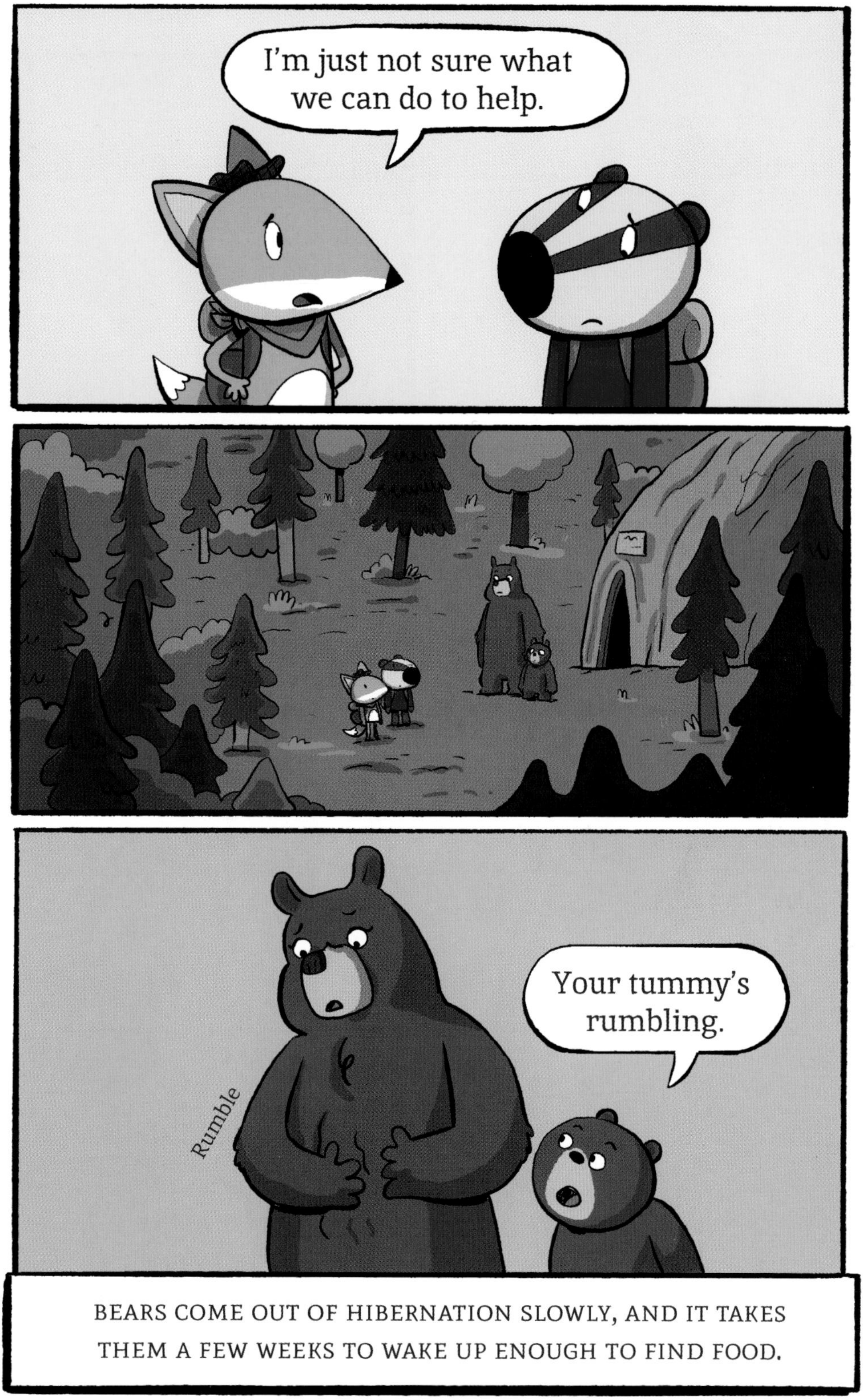
I'm just not sure what we can do to help.
Rumble
Your tummy's rumbling.
BEARS COME OUT OF HIBERNATION SLOWLY, AND IT TAKES THEM A FEW WEEKS TO WAKE UP ENOUGH TO FIND FOOD.

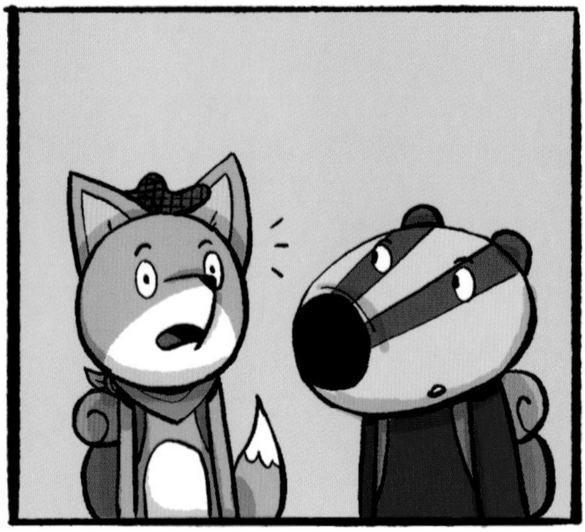

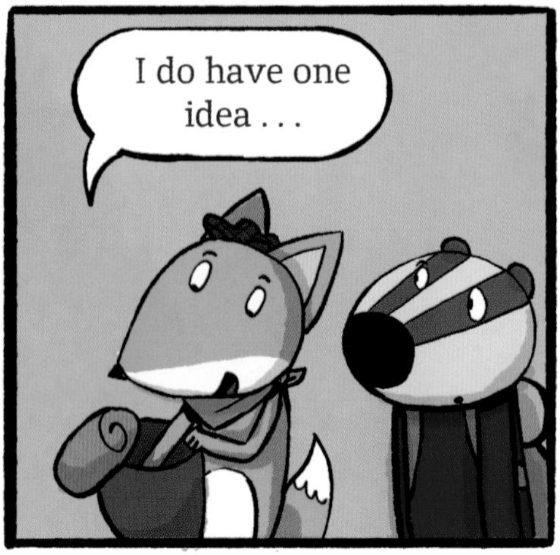
I do have one idea . . .

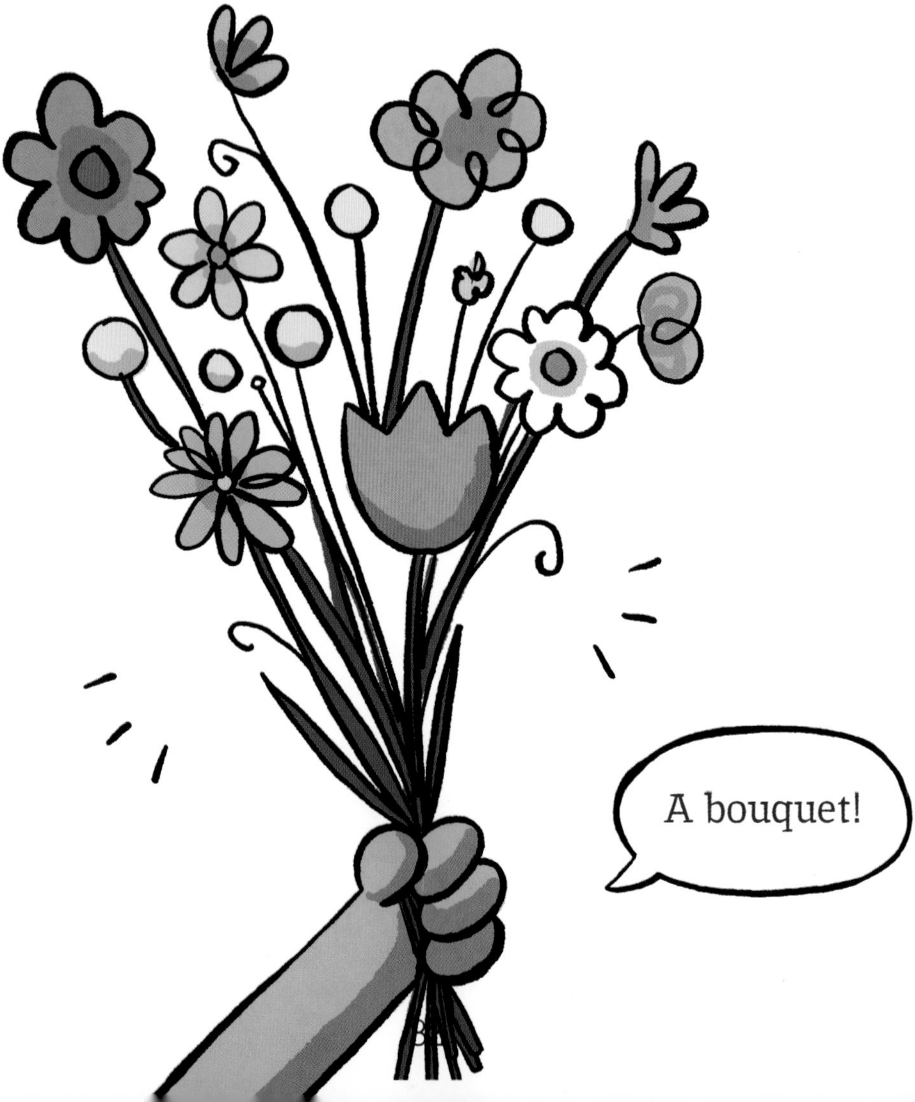
A bouquet!

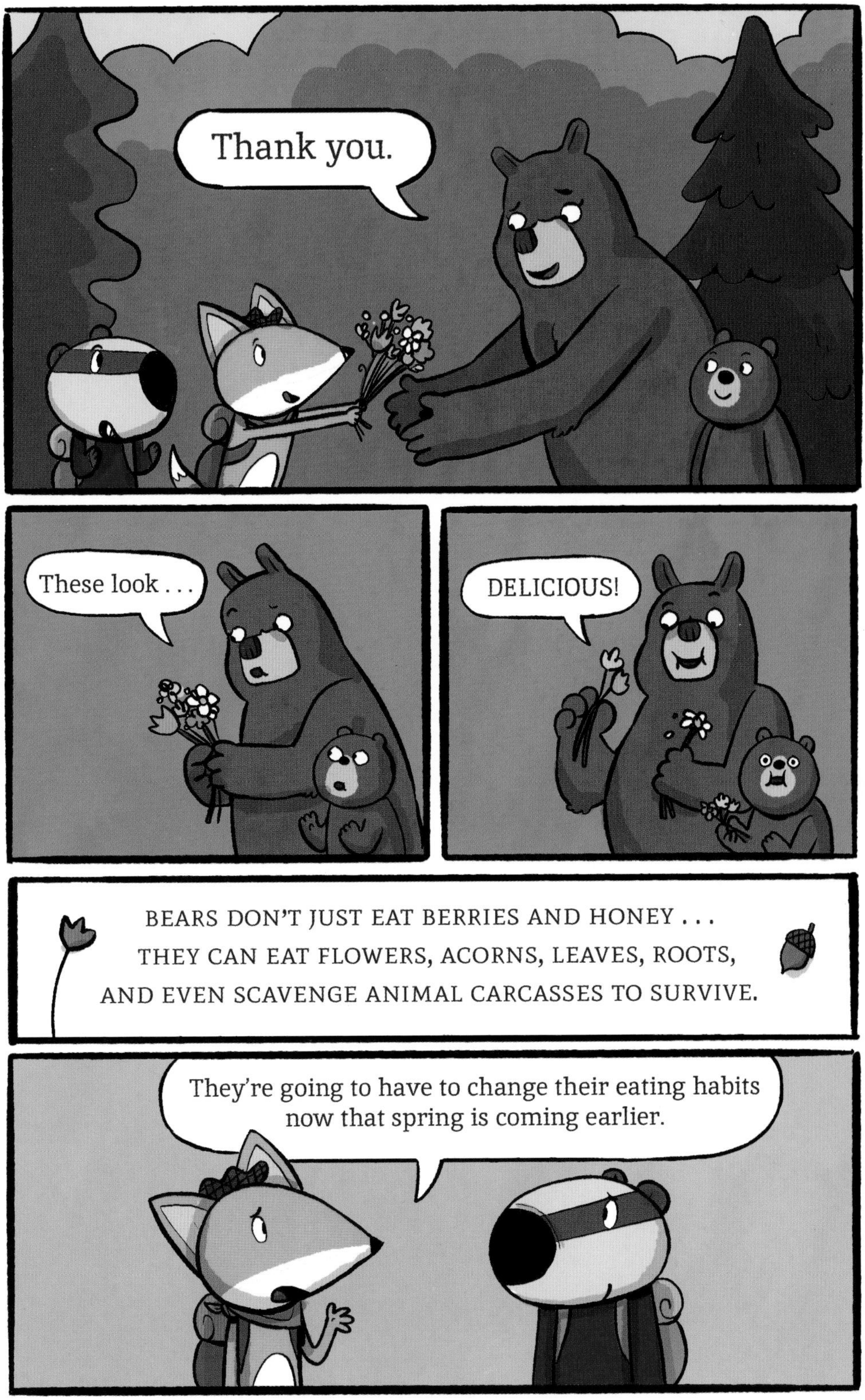
Thank you.
These look . . .
DELICIOUS!
BEARS DON'T JUST EAT BERRIES AND HONEY . . . THEY CAN EAT FLOWERS, ACORNS, LEAVES, ROOTS, AND EVEN SCAVENGE ANIMAL CARCASSES TO SURVIVE.
They're going to have to change their eating habits now that spring is coming earlier.

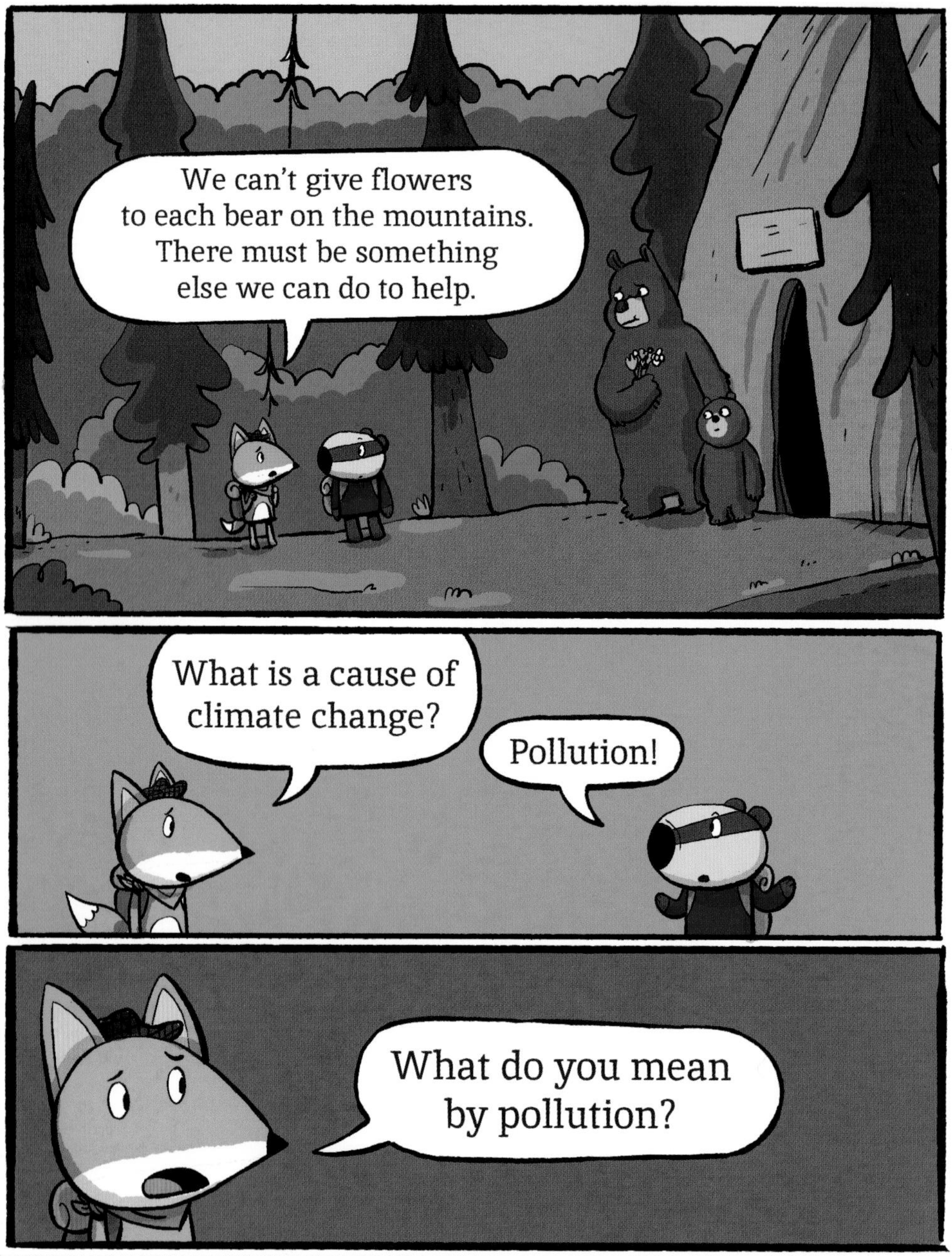
We can't give flowers to each bear on the mountains. There must be something else we can do to help.
What is a cause of climate change?
Pollution!
What do you mean by pollution?

POLLUTION: HARMFUL THINGS LIKE SMOKE OR CHEMICALS THAT ARE INTRODUCED INTO IN AN ENVIROMENT. THOSE THINGS ARE CALLED "POLLUTANTS."

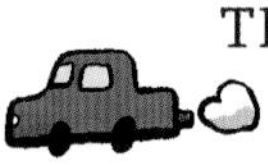

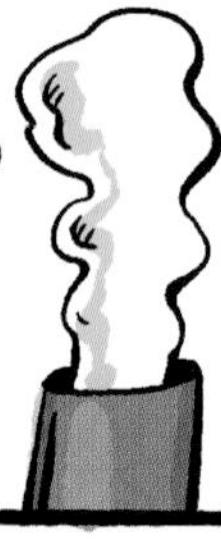

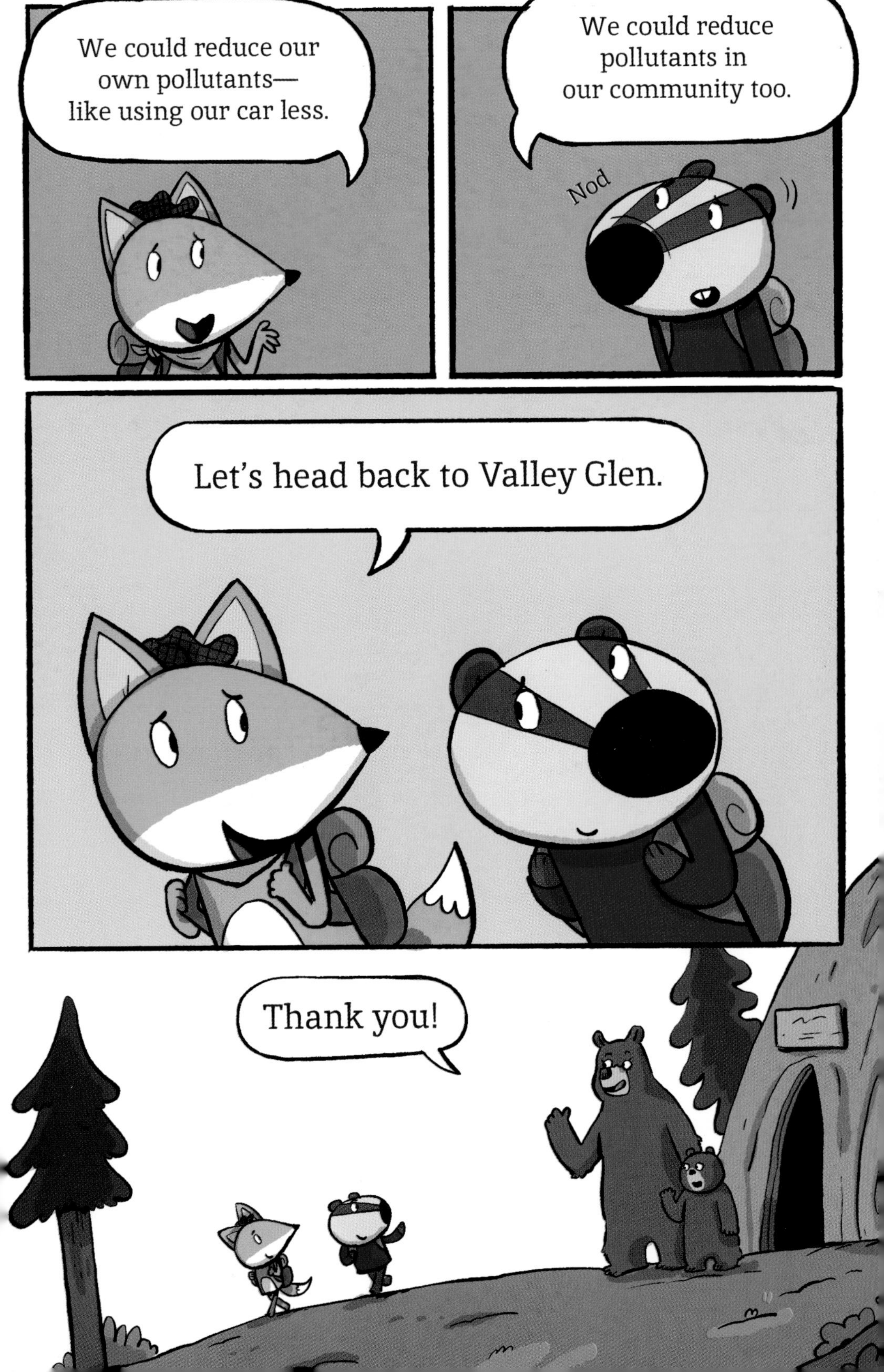
We could reduce our own pollutants—like using our car less.
We could reduce pollutants in our community too.
Nod
Let's head back to Valley Glen.
Thank you!

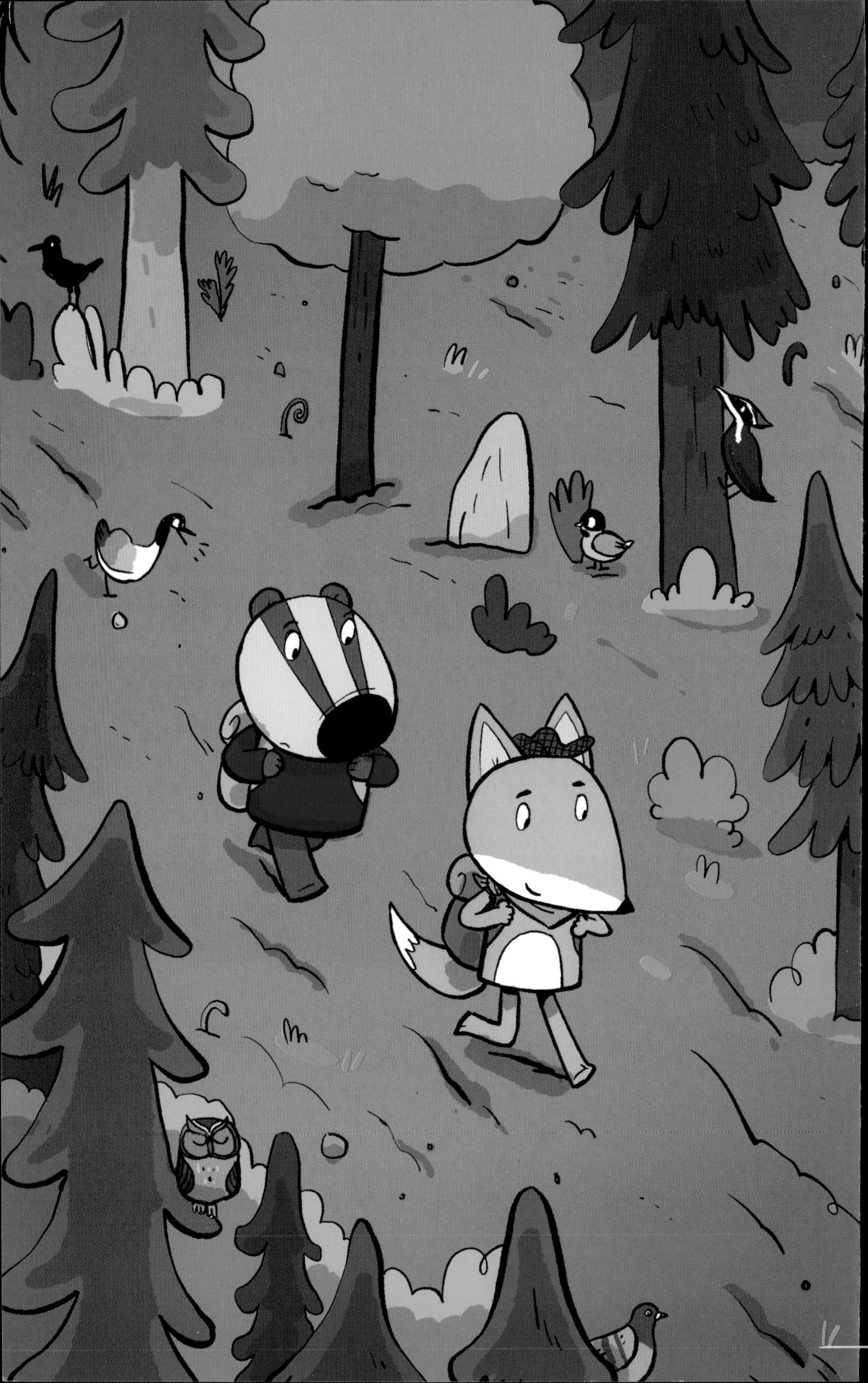

CHAPTER 7

Back to Valley Glen . . .

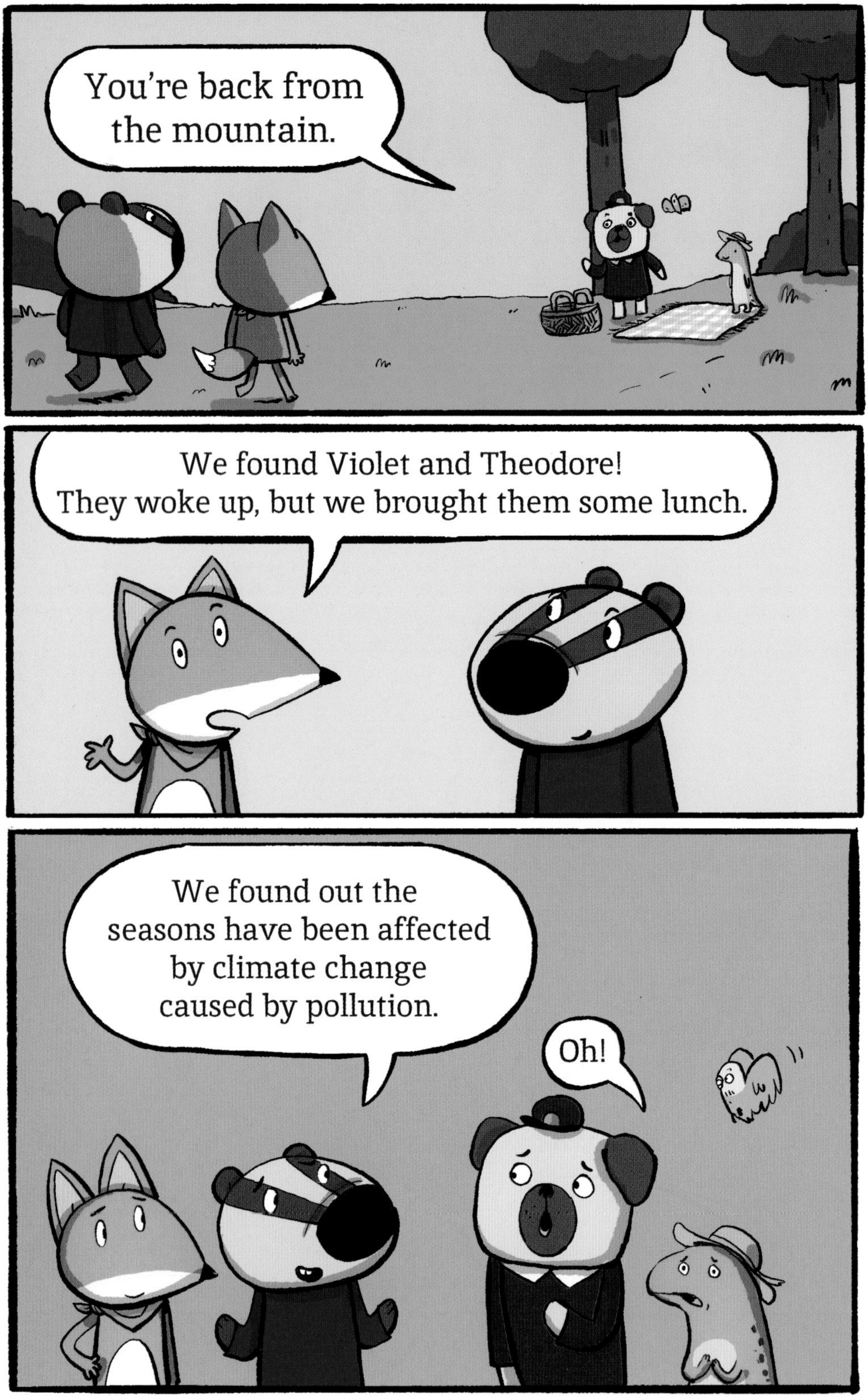
You're back from the mountain.
We found Violet and Theodore! They woke up, but we brought them some lunch.
We found out the seasons have been affected by climate change caused by pollution.
Oh!

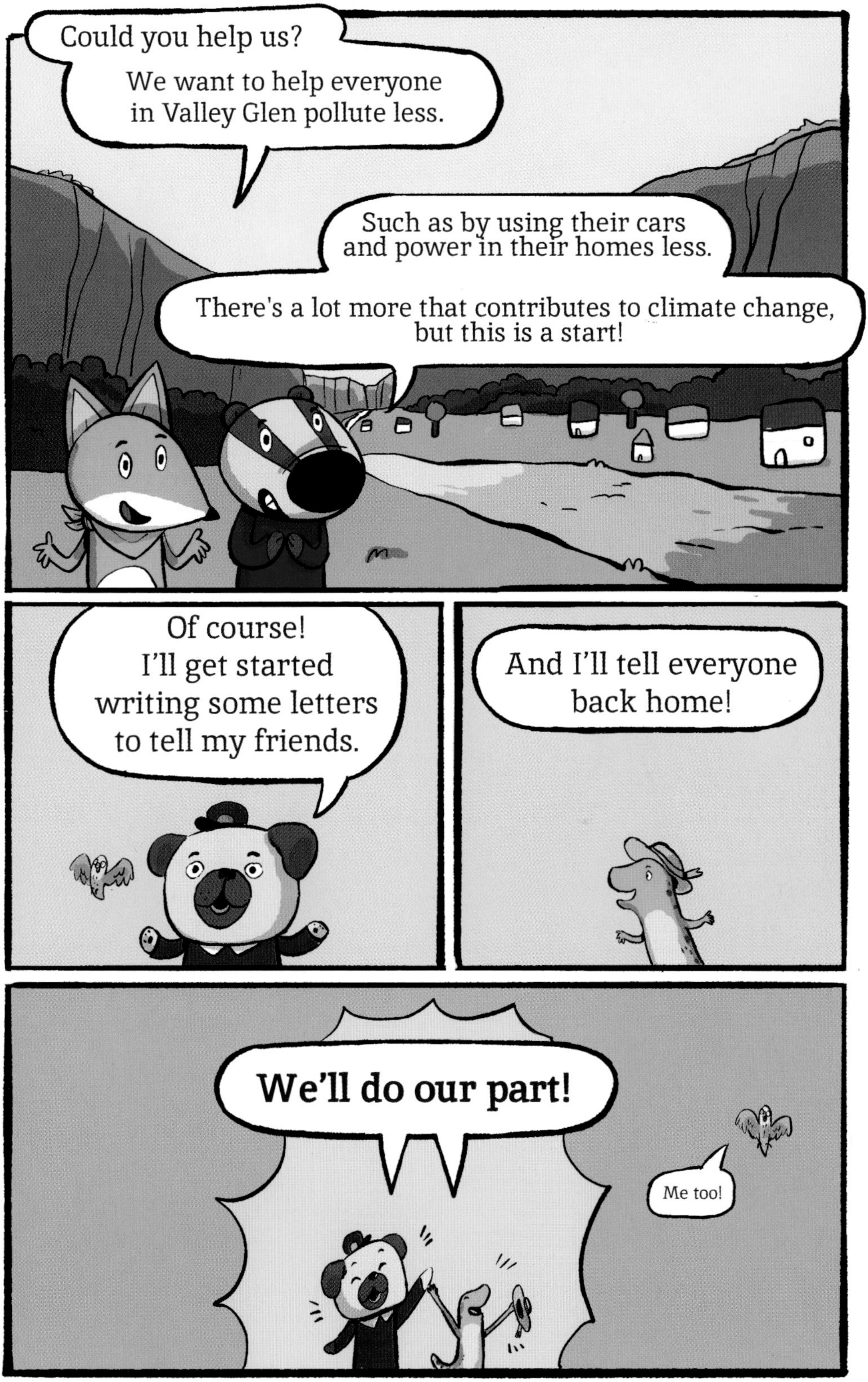
Could you help us?
We want to help everyone in Valley Glen pollute less.
Such as by using their cars and power in their homes less.
There's a lot more that contributes to climate change, but this is a start!
Of course! I'll get started writing some letters to tell my friends.
And I'll tell everyone back home!
We'll do our part!
Me too!

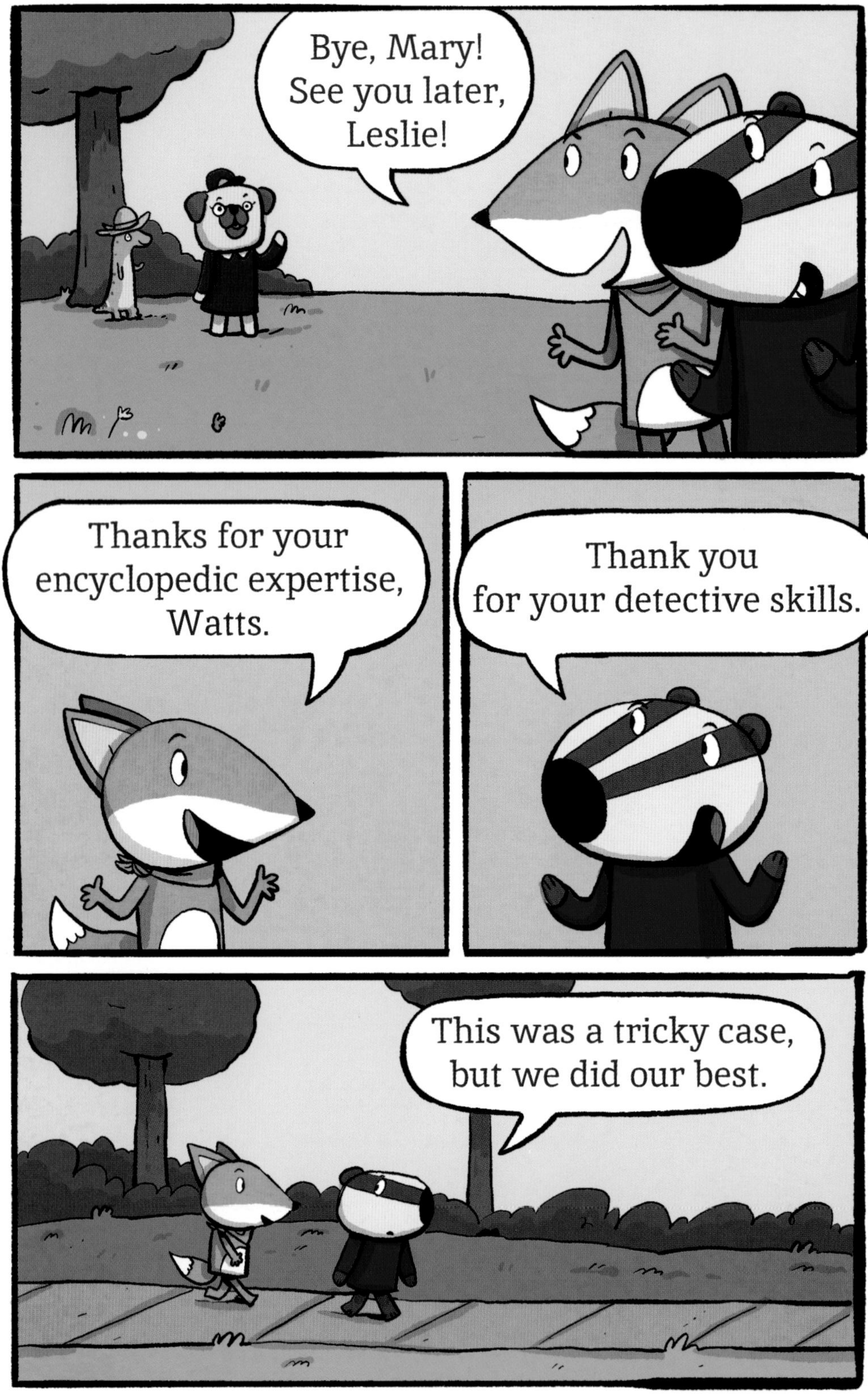
Bye, Mary! See you later, Leslie!
Thanks for your encyclopedic expertise, Watts.
Thank you for your detective skills.
This was a tricky case, but we did our best.

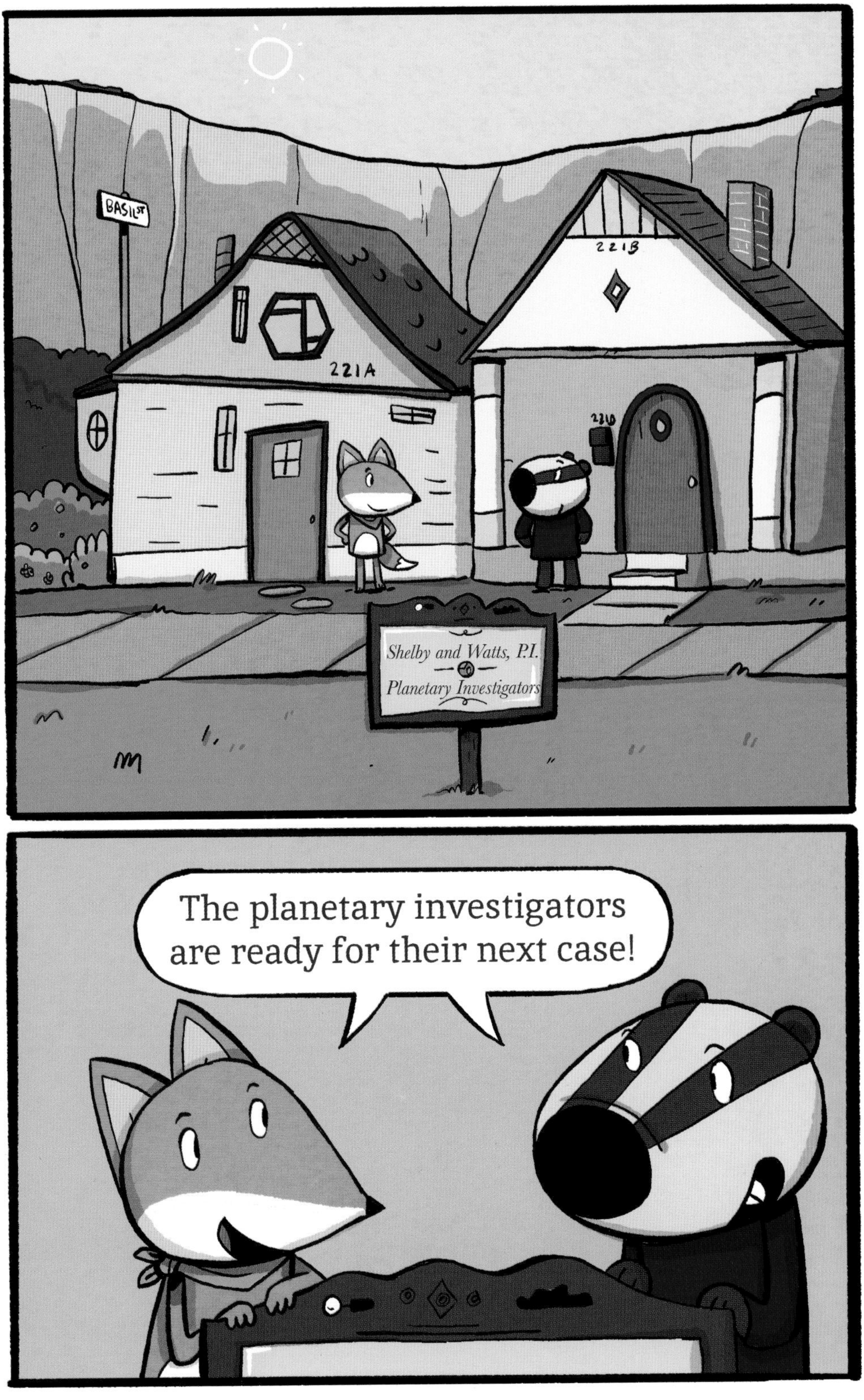
BASIL ST
221A
221B
Shelby and Watts, P.I.
Planetary Investigators
The planetary investigators are ready for their next case!

☙ Earth-Saving Tips ☙ from Shelby & Watts

Plant a tree in your community!
Plants help remove greenhouse gases
from our atmosphere.

Start a conversation about climate change.
Fear stops people from talking about it,
but learning more about it is the best way to beat it.

Talk to your family, friends, and community
about using cars and other energy sources less.

Carpool!

Turn off lights!

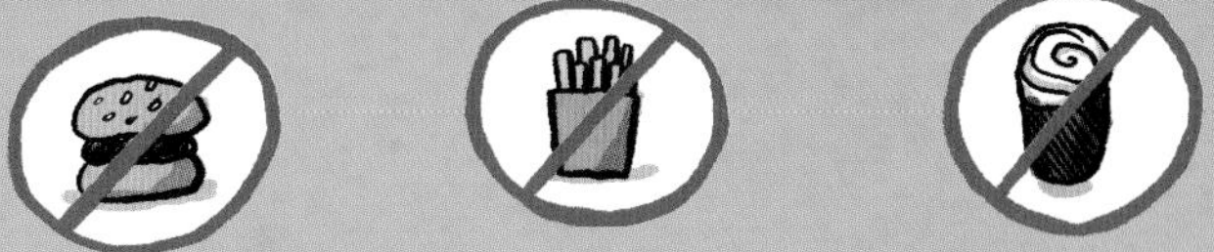

If you see a bear coming out of hibernation early, don't feed it human food! It will find food in its environment.

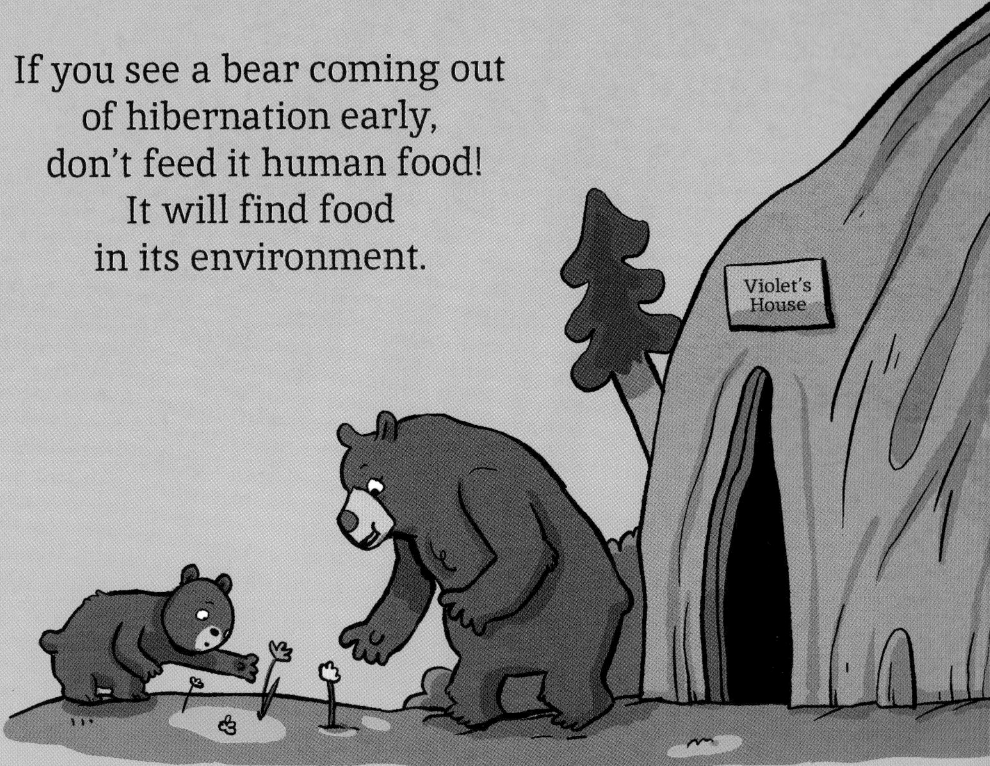
Violet's House

Factories, businesses, and corporations are another big source of pollution. You can write letters to your community leaders about creating new laws or practices to protect our planet.

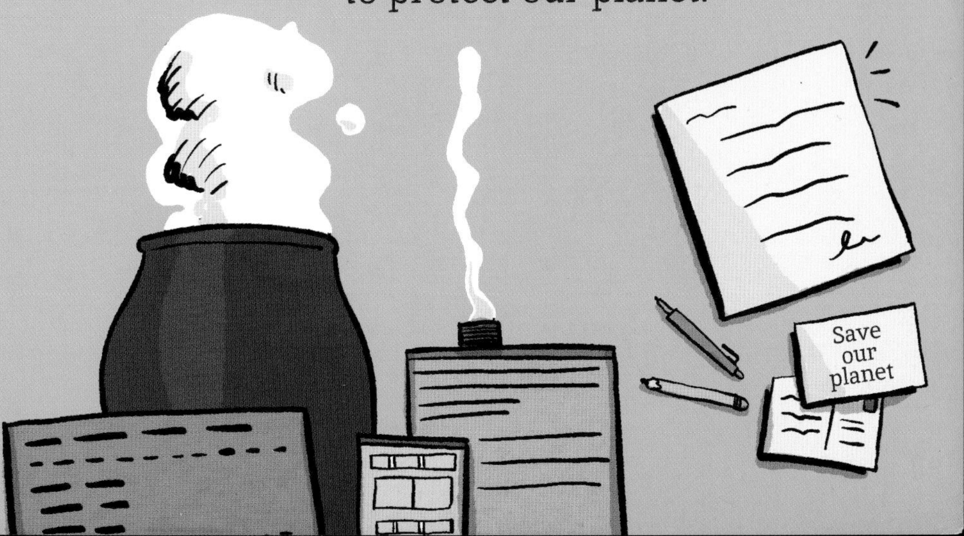
Save our planet

Ashlyn Anstee grew up in a rainy city in Canada and then settled in a sunny city in the United States with her husband and four cats. She works in the animation industry and, in her spare time, drinks tea and takes naps. She writes, draws, illustrates, animates, and is the creator of the books *No, No, Gnome!*, *Are We There, Yeti?*, and *Hedgehog!*

A Mountain of a Problem is the follow-up to her first Shelby and Watts graphic novel, *Tide Pool Troubles*. Find out more at ashlyna.com.